LEWIS CARROLL'S

# ALICE
## IN WONDERLAND

A GRAPHIC NOVEL

BY MARTIN POWELL &
DANIEL FERRAN

STONE ARCH BOOKS
A CAPSTONE IMPRINT

Graphic Revolve is published by Stone Arch Books
A Capstone Imprint
1710 Roe Crest Drive, North Mankato, Minnesota 56003
www.capstonepub.com



Cataloging-in-Publication Data is available at the Library of Congress website.
Hardcover ISBN: 978-1-4965-0021-2
Paperback ISBN: 978-1-4965-0040-3

Summary: A girl named Alice suddenly spots a frantic White Rabbit. She follows the hurried creature into the magical world of Wonderland. While there, Alice meets more crazy creatures and plays a twisted game of croquet with the Queen of Hearts. But when the Queen turns against her, this dream-like world becomes a nightmare.

Common Core back matter written by Dr. Katie Monnin.

Color by Sebastian Facio and Daniel Ferran.

Designer: Bob Lentz
Assistant Designer: Peggie Carley
Editor: Donald Lemke
Assistant Editor: Sean Tulien
Creative Director: Heather Kindseth
Editorial Director: Michael Dahl
Publisher: Ashley C. Andersen Zantop

Printed in the United States of America.
3016

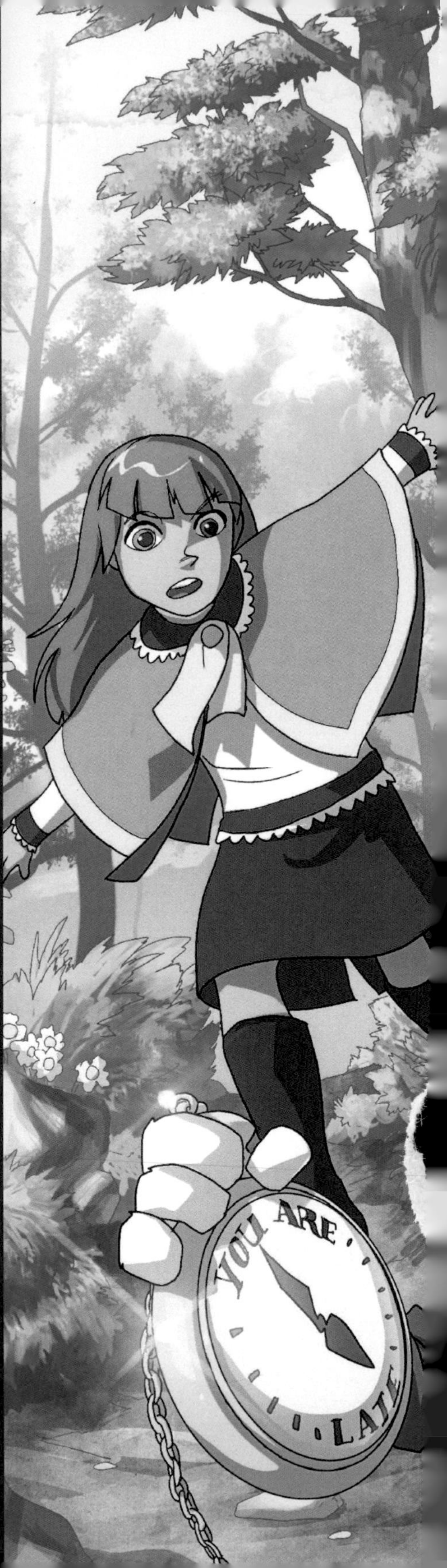
YOU ARE
LATE

# TABLE OF CONTENTS

# THE WORLD OF LEWIS CARROLL

In 1856, Charles Lutwidge Dodgson, also known as Lewis Carroll, met three young children named Edith, Lorina, and Alice Liddell. One day, he took them on a trip in a rowboat. Carroll devised a silly story on the spot as they paddled down the river. Young Alice loved the story so much that she asked Carroll to write it down for her. Just like that, the idea for *The Adventures of Alice in Wonderland* was born. Here are some other interesting facts from the famous tale . . .

Hatters, or hat makers, were considered to be "mad," or crazy, because they used mercury in the production of hats. They regularly touched the mercury, which often led to brain damage from mercury poisoning. In *Wonderland*, the Mad Hatter is the host of a tea party that never ends. His guests are the sleepy Dormouse and the March Hare. The "10/6" card that sits in his hat is a price tag that hatters used in their shops. The hat he wears would have sold for ten shillings and six pence in Lewis Carroll's day. That's about one hundred American dollars today — so it was probably a very nice hat.

"Dormouse" comes from the word "dormeus," which means "sleepy one." Dormice have very strange sleep patterns. They hibernate up to six months out of every year. They often wake up and eat, then slip back into hibernation. Despite their sleepy tendencies, they are very agile and well-suited for climbing and jumping. In *Wonderland*, the Dormouse is a creature who sleeps through most of the Mad Hatter's tea party.

Some cheeses from Cheshire county, Lewis Carroll's home town, were molded in the shape of a grinning cat. They were known as Cheshire Cat cheeses, and they were cut from the tail end first, leaving the head for last. In Alice, this is a lot like how the Cheshire Cat vanishes, leaving only its smiling face behind. It is believed this is why Carroll chose to name the strange feline featured in the tale.

# CAST OF CHARACTERS

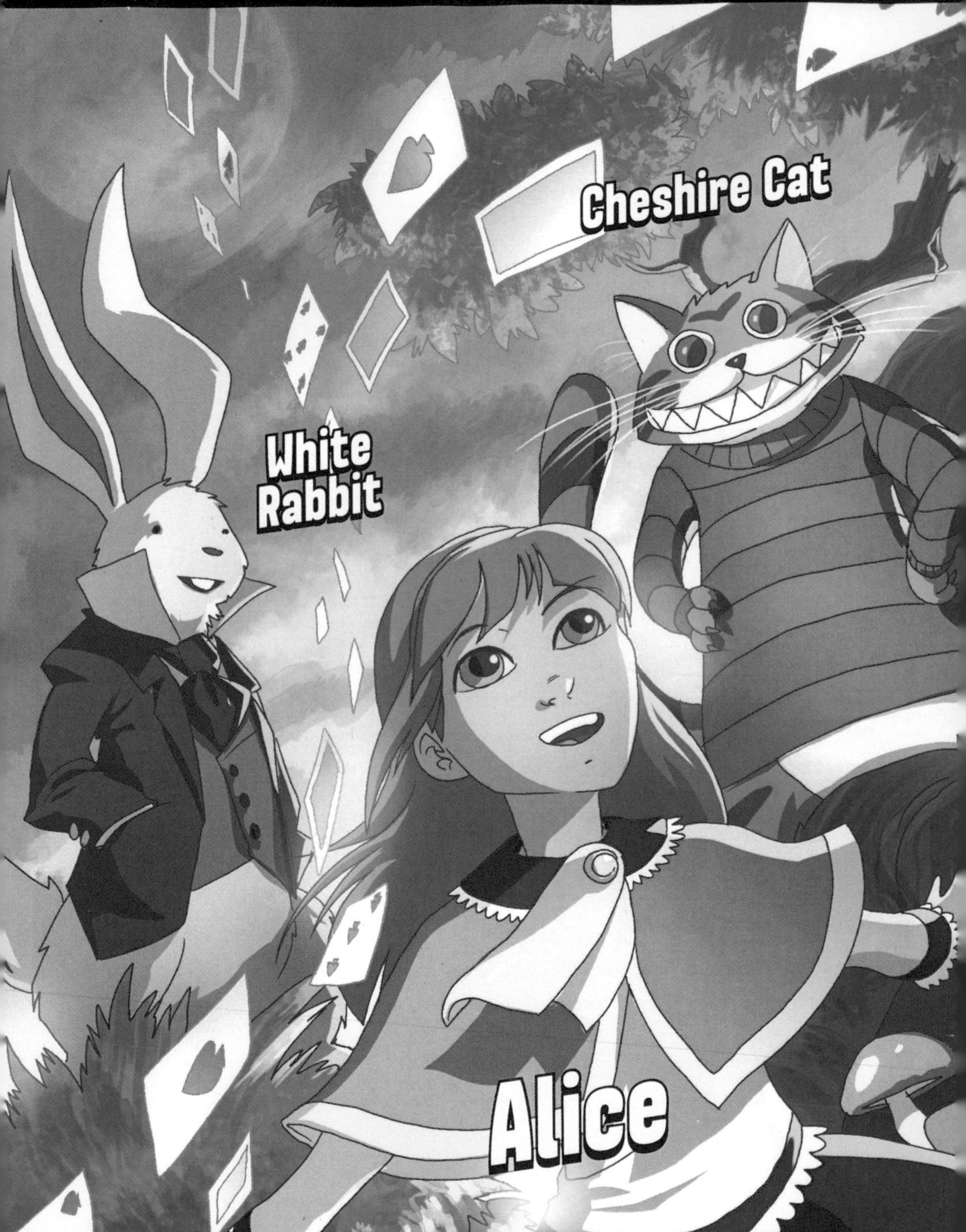
Cheshire Cat
White Rabbit
Alice

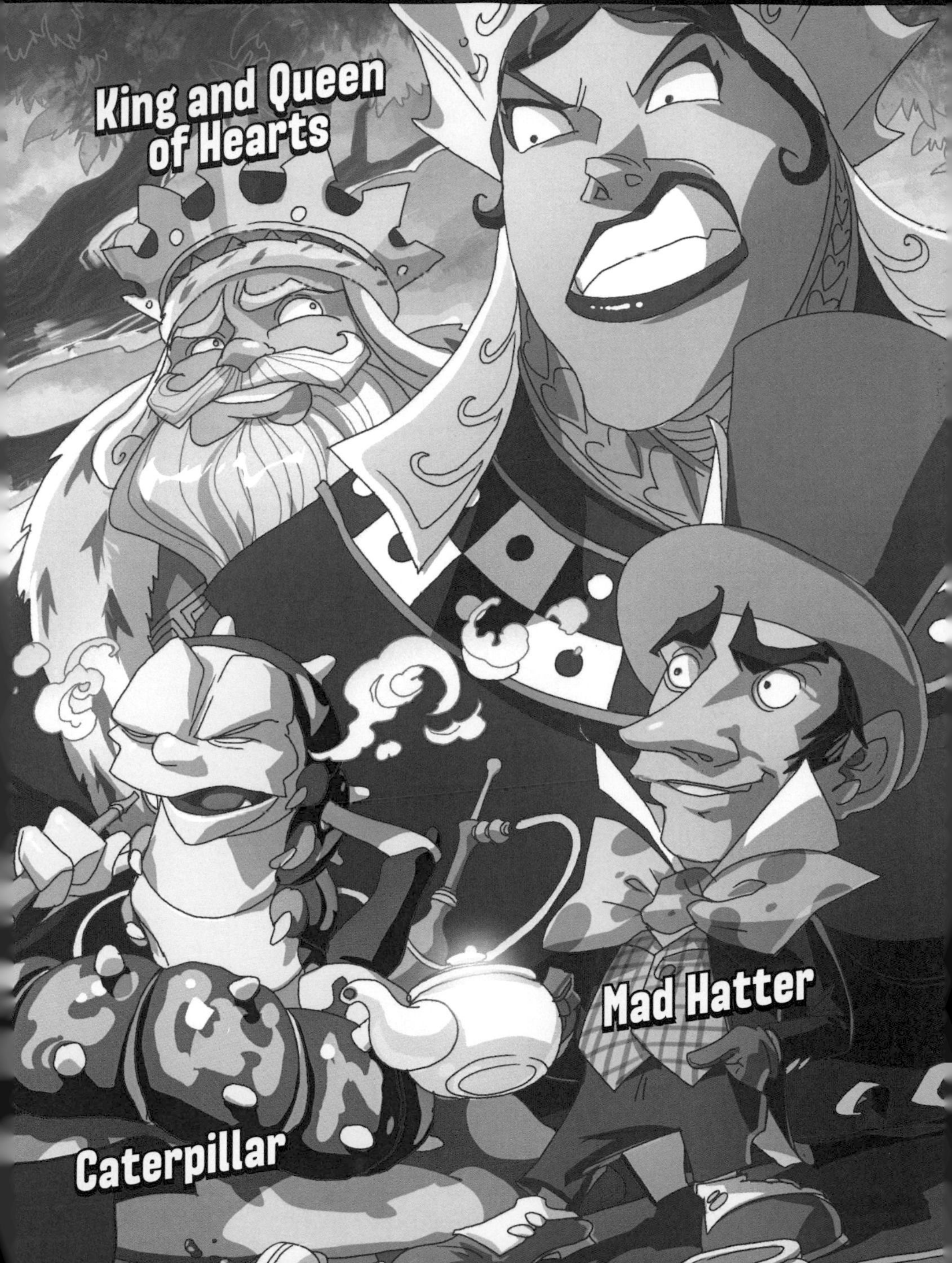
King and Queen of Hearts
Mad Hatter
Caterpillar

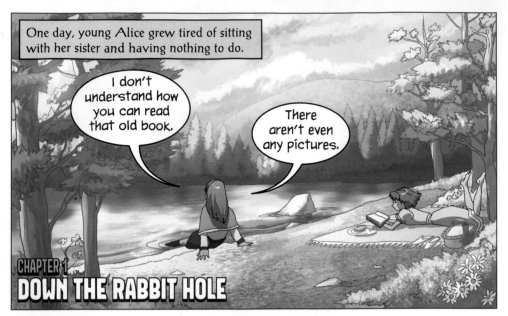

One day, young Alice grew tired of sitting with her sister and having nothing to do.

I don't understand how you can read that old book.

There aren't even any pictures.

CHAPTER 1

# DOWN THE RABBIT HOLE

What good is a book without pictures?

I'd make a chain of daisies, if I wasn't feeling so lazy and so —

Why, it's a rabbit . . .

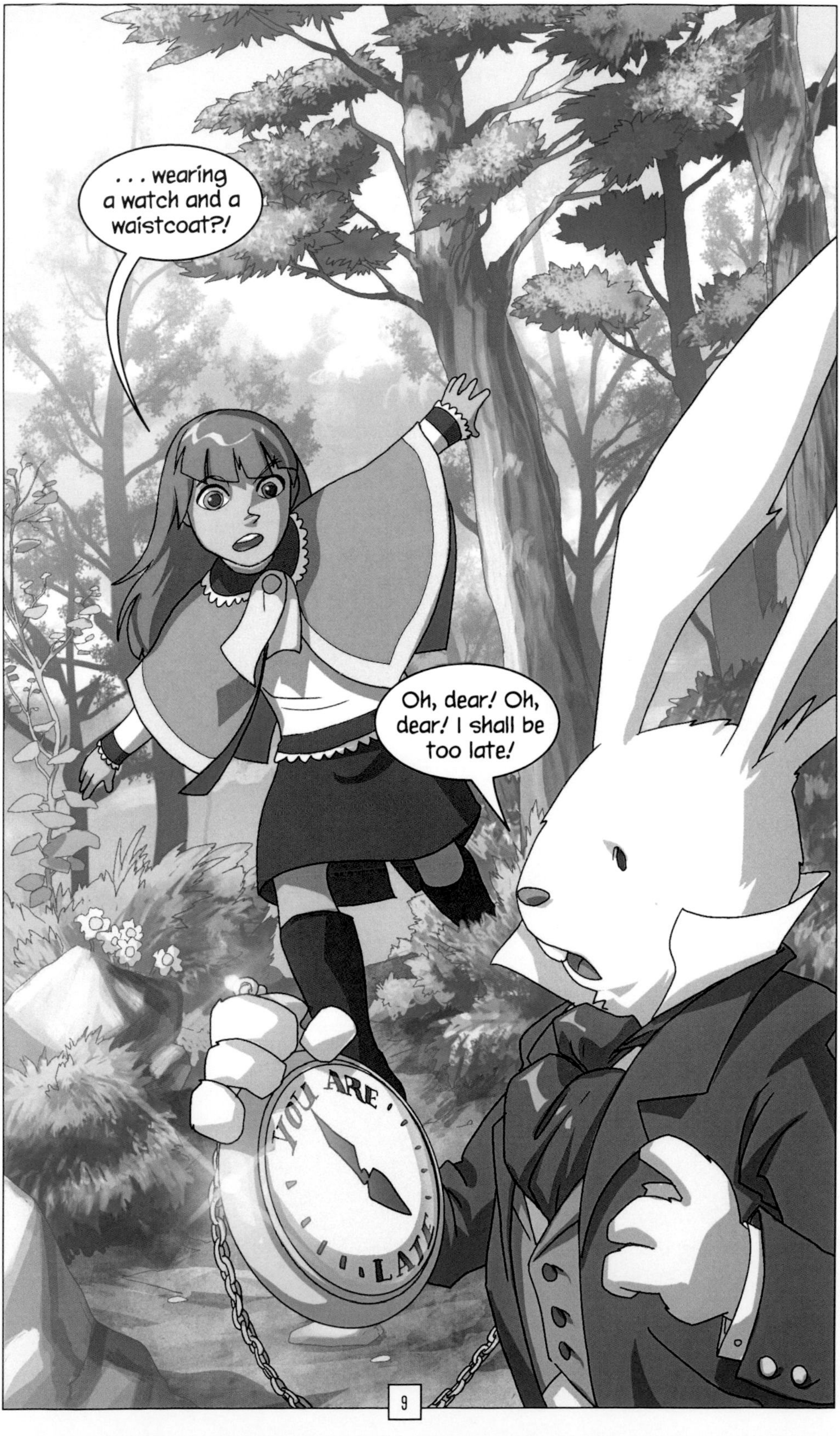
. . . wearing a watch and a waistcoat?!
Oh, dear! Oh, dear! I shall be too late!
YOU ARE LATE

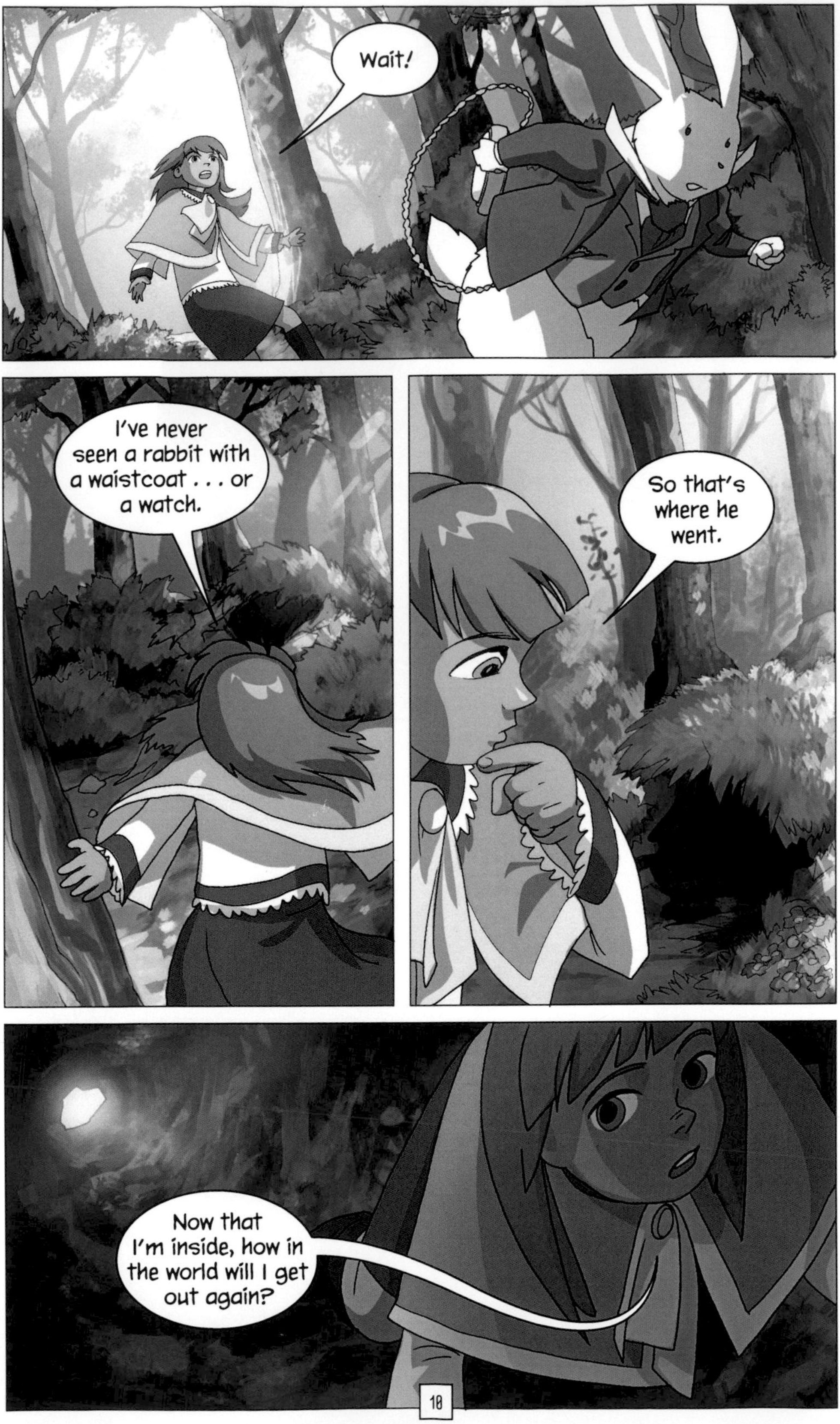
Wait!
I've never seen a rabbit with a waistcoat . . . or a watch.
So that's where he went.
Now that I'm inside, how in the world will I get out again?

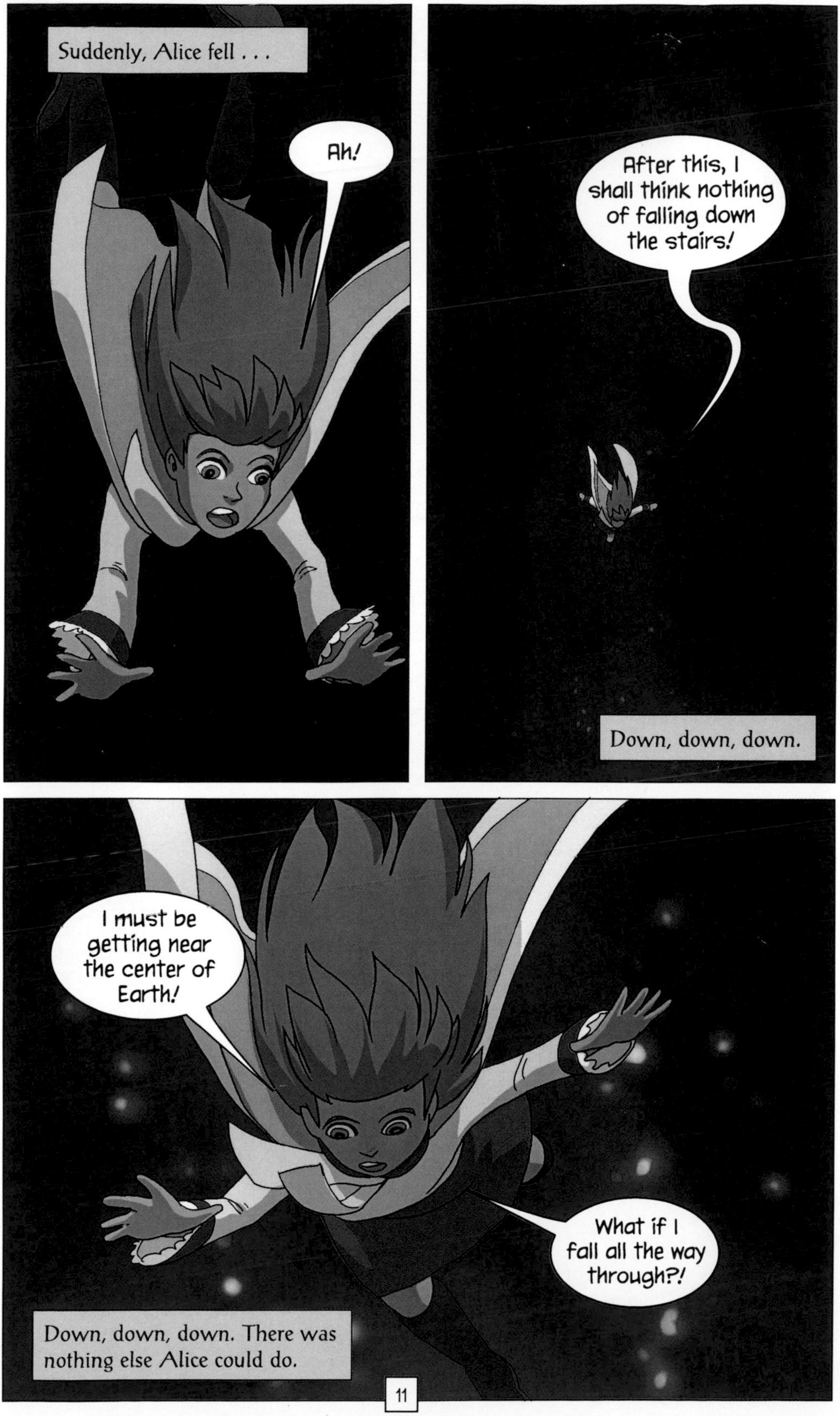
Suddenly, Alice fell . . .
Ah!
After this, I shall think nothing of falling down the stairs!
Down, down, down.
I must be getting near the center of Earth!
What if I fall all the way through?!
Down, down, down. There was nothing else Alice could do.

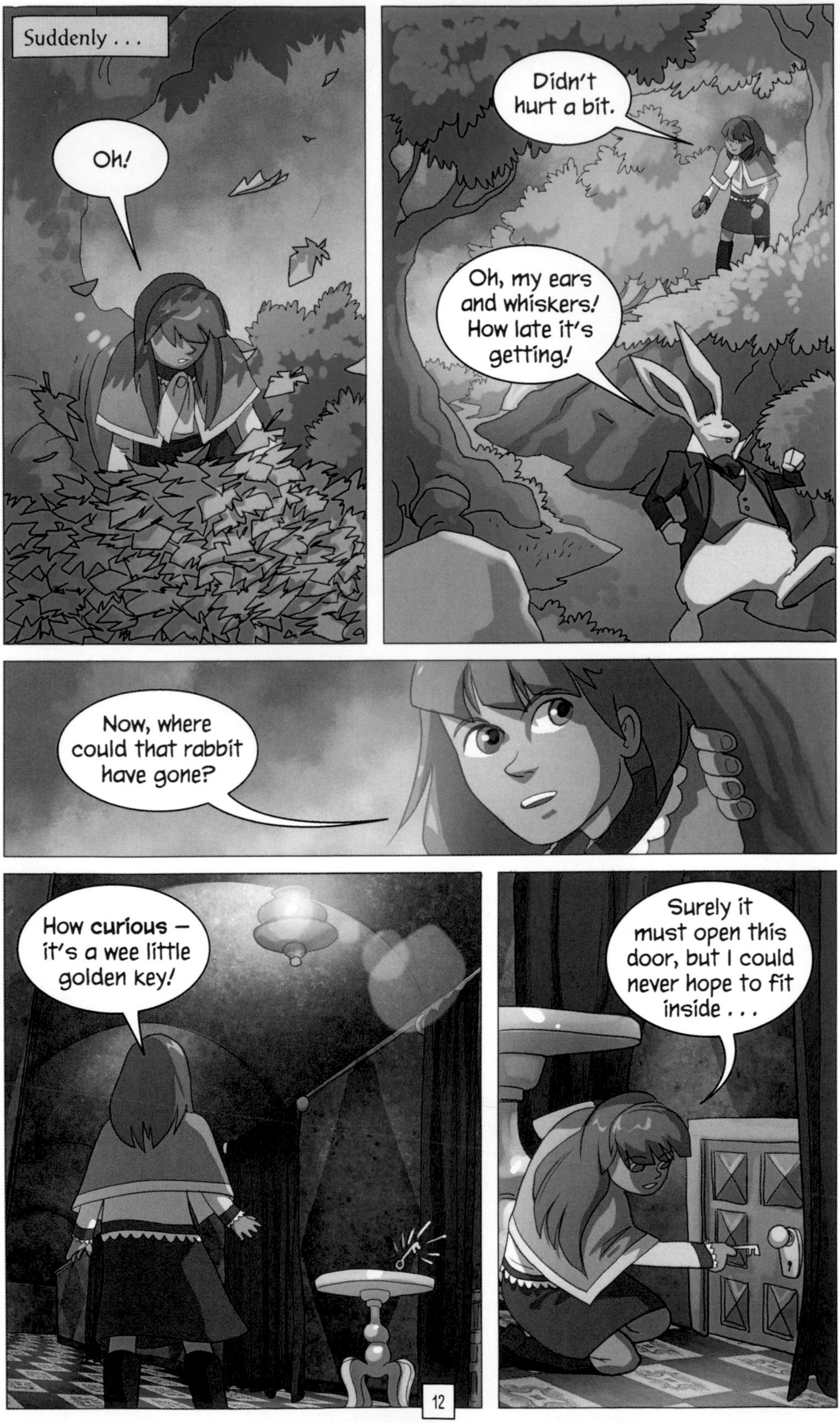
Suddenly . . .
Oh!
Didn't hurt a bit.
Oh, my ears and whiskers! How late it's getting!
Now, where could that rabbit have gone?
How **curious** – it's a wee little golden key!
Surely it must open this door, but I could never hope to fit inside . . .

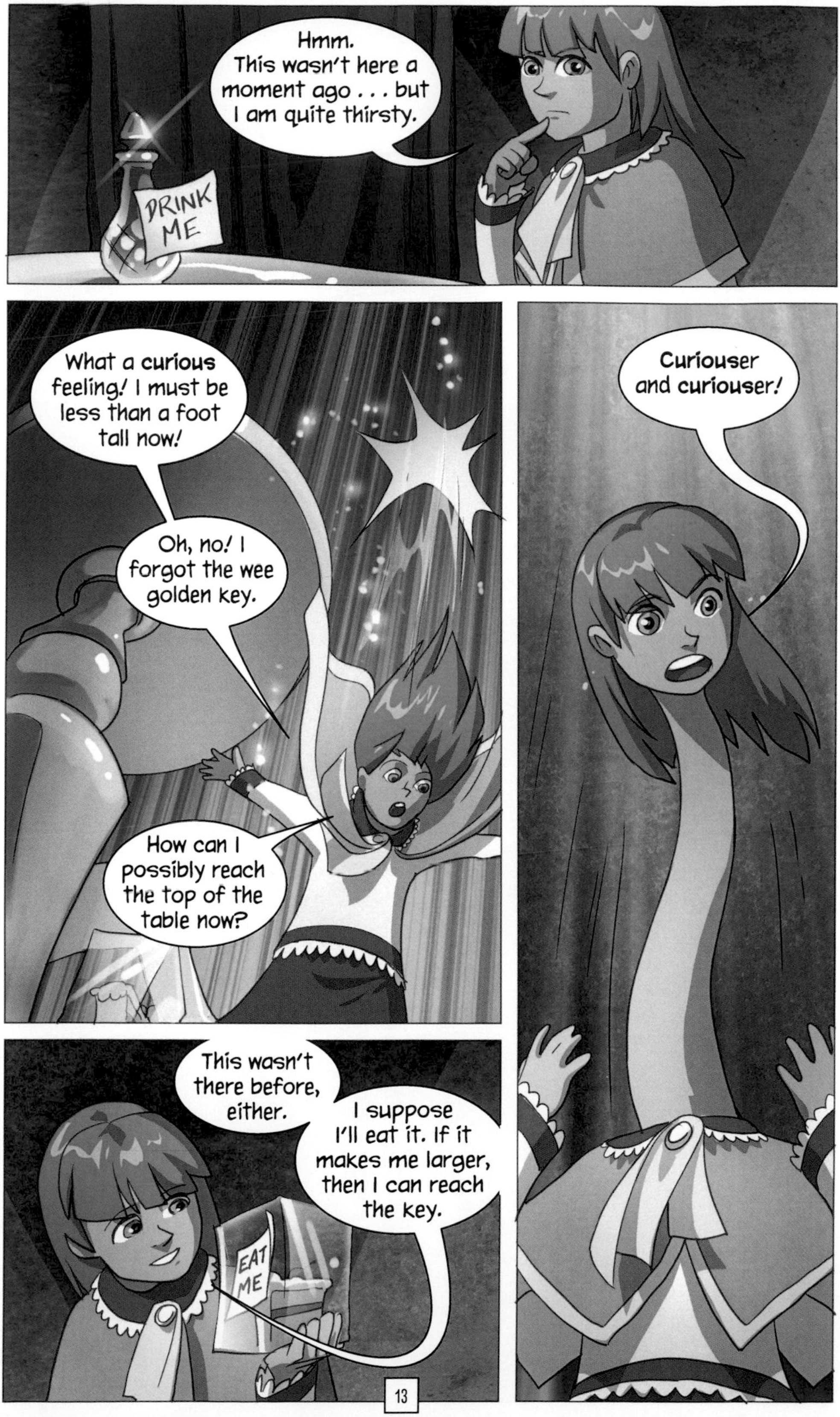
Hmm. This wasn't here a moment ago . . . but I am quite thirsty.
DRINK ME
What a **curious** feeling! I must be less than a foot tall now!
Oh, no! I forgot the wee golden key.
How can I possibly reach the top of the table now?
**Curiouser** and **curiouser**!
This wasn't there before, either.
I suppose I'll eat it. If it makes me larger, then I can reach the key.
EAT ME

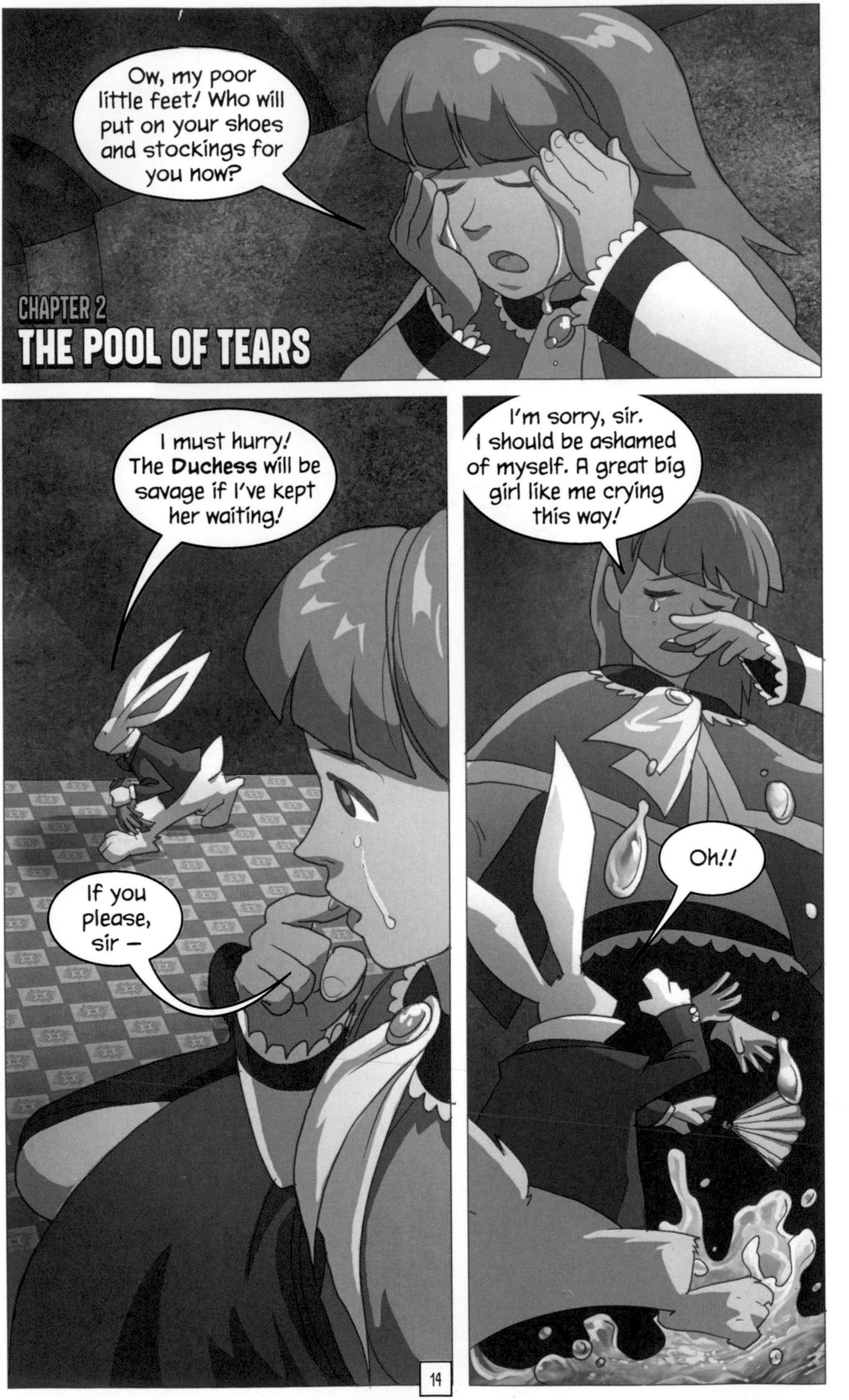
Ow, my poor little feet! Who will put on your shoes and stockings for you now?
CHAPTER 2
THE POOL OF TEARS
I must hurry! The Duchess will be savage if I've kept her waiting!
If you please, sir —
I'm sorry, sir. I should be ashamed of myself. A great big girl like me crying this way!
Oh!!

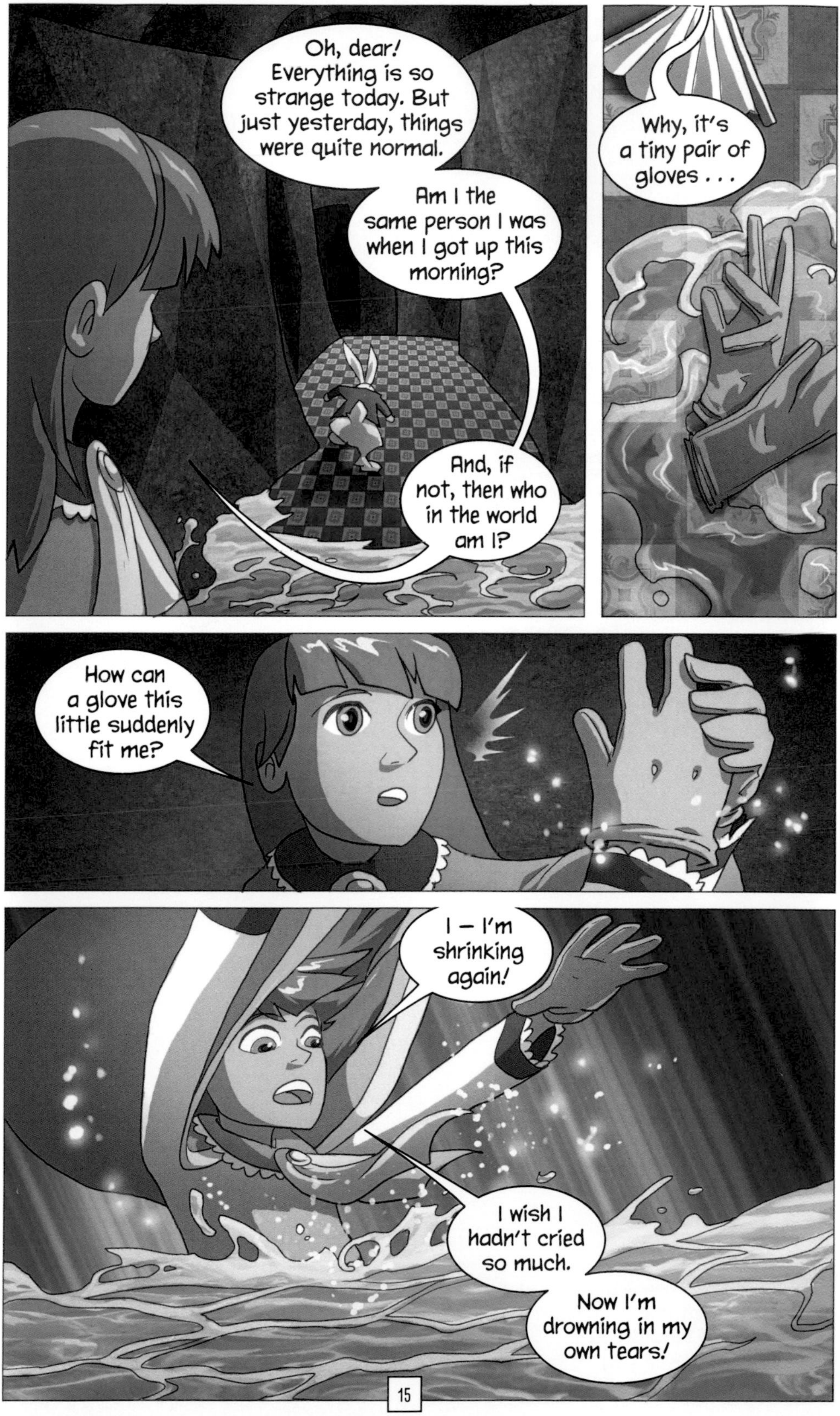
Oh, dear! Everything is so strange today. But just yesterday, things were quite normal.
Am I the same person I was when I got up this morning?
And, if not, then who in the world am I?
Why, it's a tiny pair of gloves . . .
How can a glove this little suddenly fit me?
I – I'm shrinking again!
I wish I hadn't cried so much.
Now I'm drowning in my own tears!

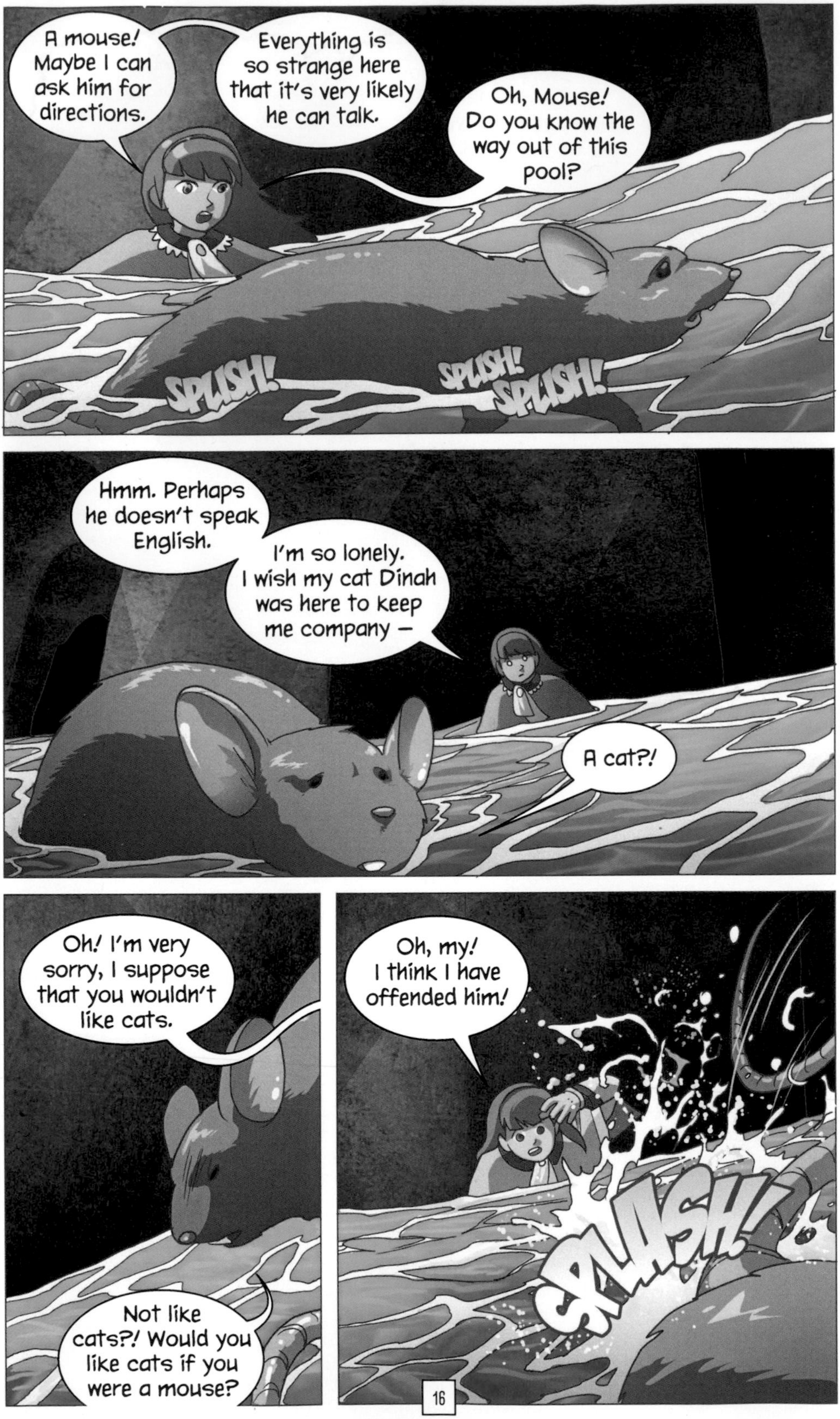
A mouse! Maybe I can ask him for directions.
Everything is so strange here that it's very likely he can talk.
Oh, Mouse! Do you know the way out of this pool?
SPLISH!
SPLISH!
SPLISH!
Hmm. Perhaps he doesn't speak English.
I'm so lonely. I wish my cat Dinah was here to keep me company –
A cat?!
Oh! I'm very sorry, I suppose that you wouldn't like cats.
Not like cats?! Would you like cats if you were a mouse?
Oh, my! I think I have offended him!
SPLASH!

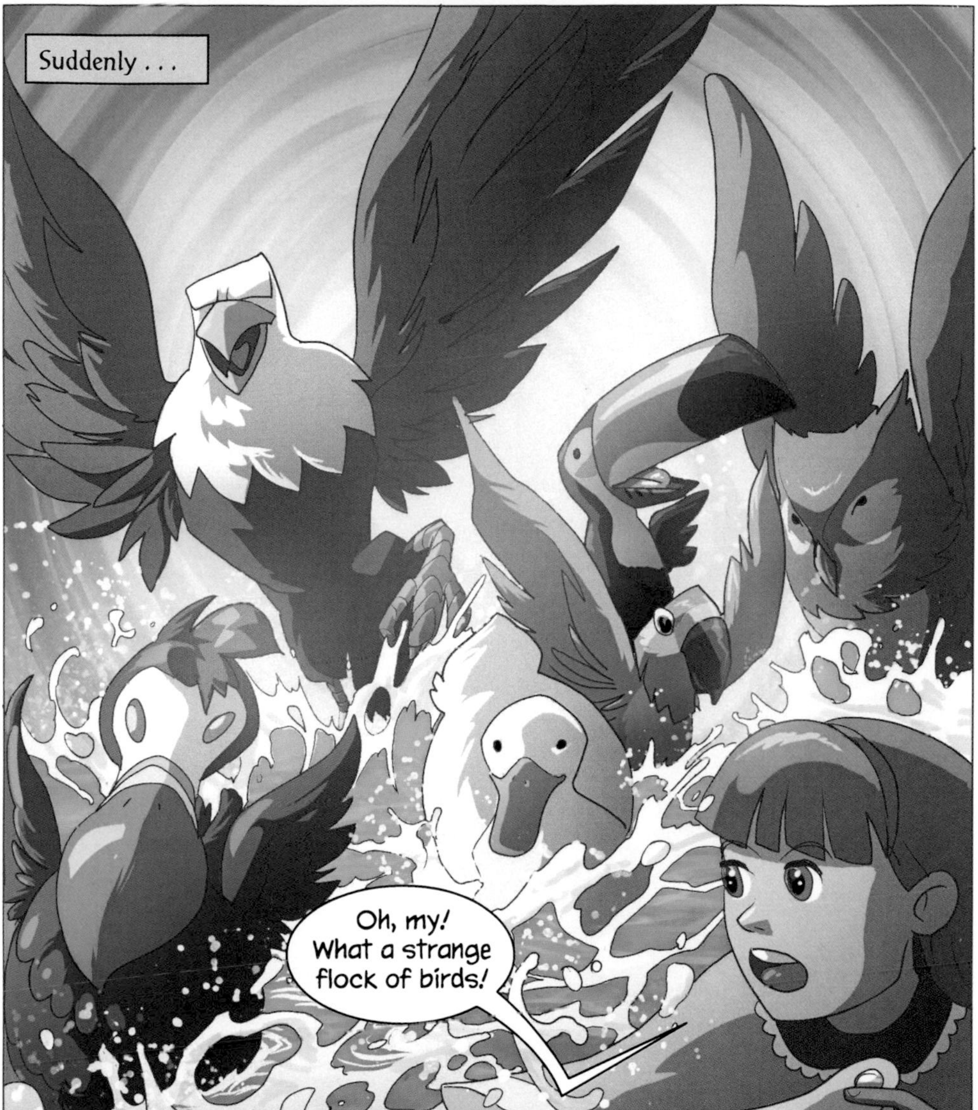
Suddenly . . .
Oh, my! What a strange flock of birds!

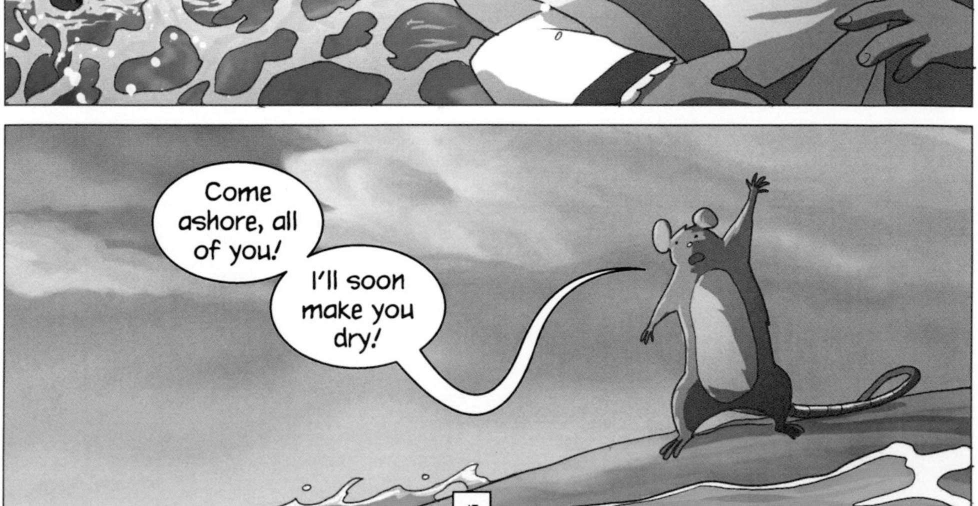
Come ashore, all of you!
I'll soon make you dry!

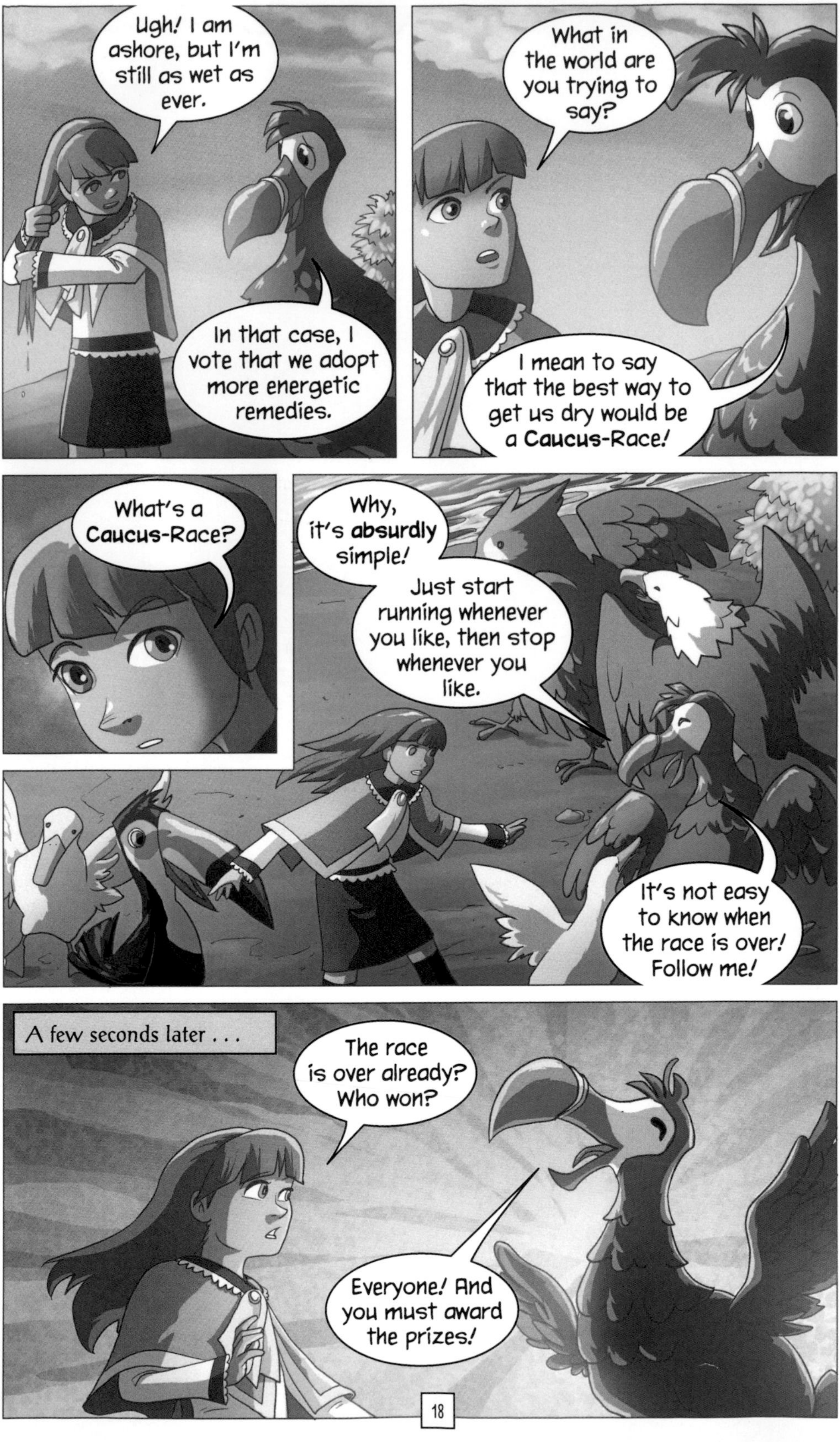
Ugh! I am ashore, but I'm still as wet as ever.
In that case, I vote that we adopt more energetic remedies.
What in the world are you trying to say?
I mean to say that the best way to get us dry would be a **Caucus-Race!**
What's a **Caucus-Race?**
Why, it's **absurdly** simple!
Just start running whenever you like, then stop whenever you like.
It's not easy to know when the race is over! Follow me!
A few seconds later . . .
The race is over already? Who won?
Everyone! And you must award the prizes!

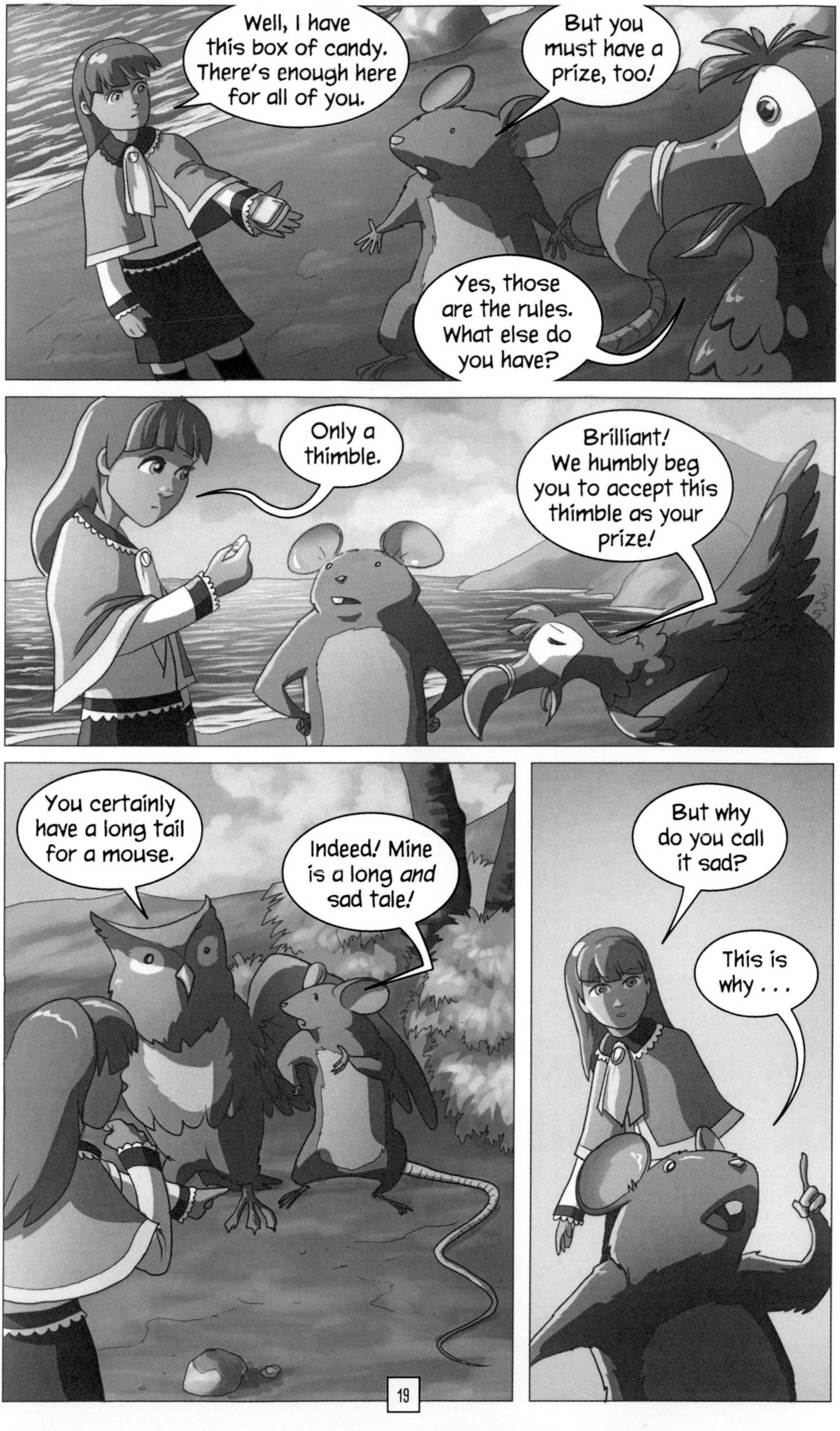
Well, I have this box of candy. There's enough here for all of you.
But you must have a prize, too!
Yes, those are the rules. What else do you have?
Only a thimble.
Brilliant! We humbly beg you to accept this thimble as your prize!
You certainly have a long tail for a mouse.
Indeed! Mine is a long *and* sad tale!
But why do you call it sad?
This is why . . .

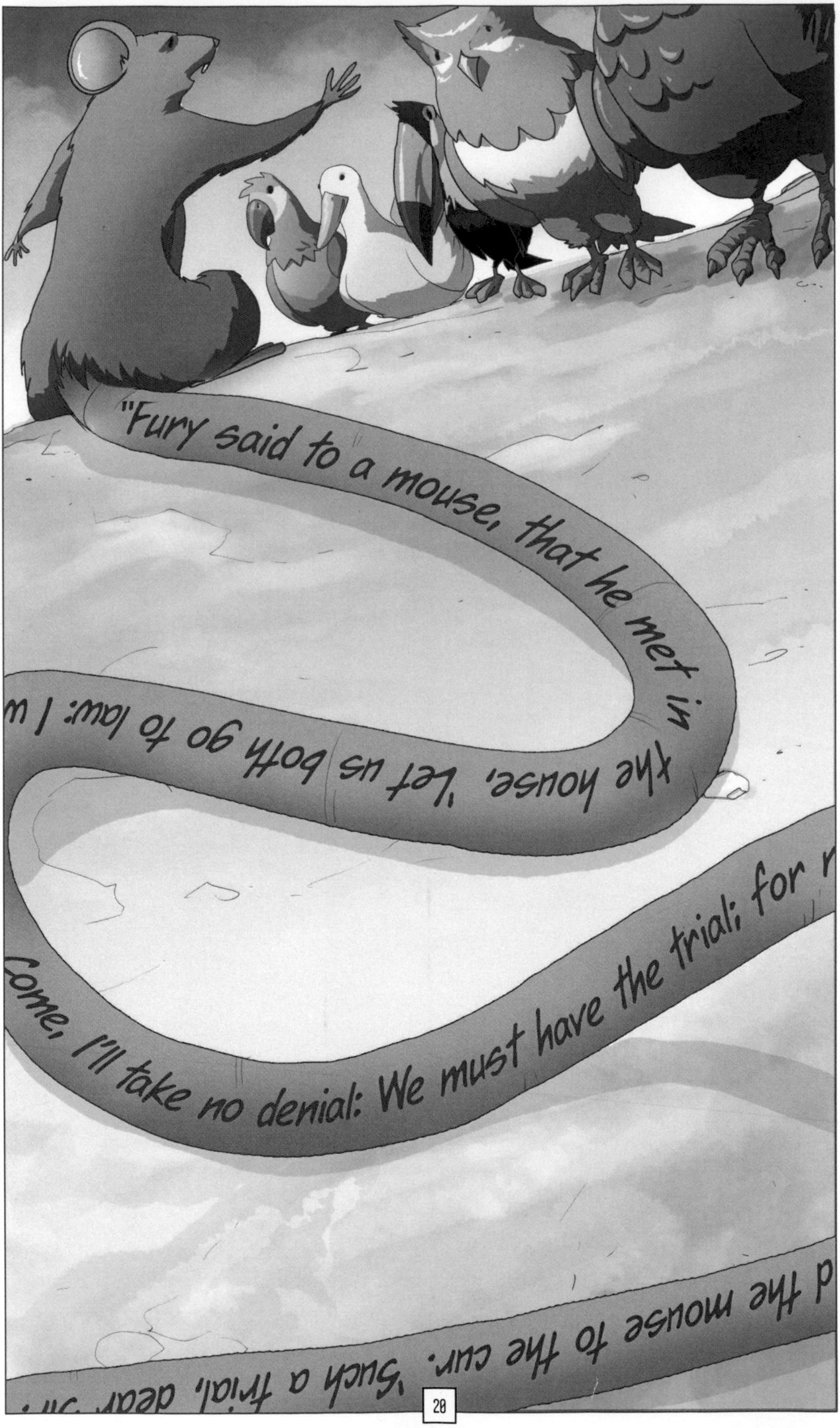
"Fury said to a mouse, that he met in the house, 'Let us both go to law: I
Come, I'll take no denial: We must have the trial: for
the mouse to the cur. 'Such a trial, dear Sir,'

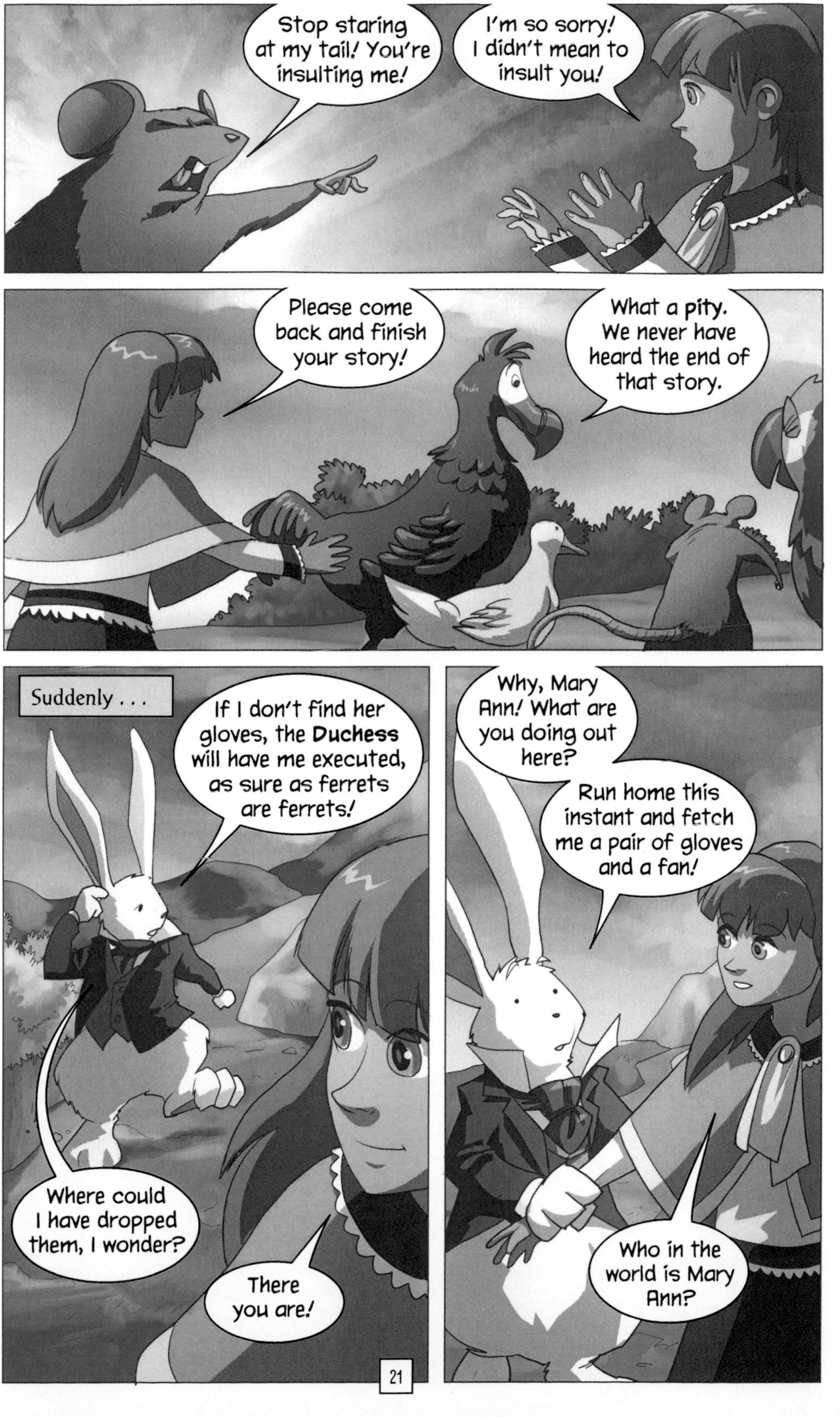
Stop staring at my tail! You're insulting me!
I'm so sorry! I didn't mean to insult you!
Please come back and finish your story!
What a pity. We never have heard the end of that story.
Suddenly . . .
If I don't find her gloves, the Duchess will have me executed, as sure as ferrets are ferrets!
Where could I have dropped them, I wonder?
There you are!
Why, Mary Ann! What are you doing out here?
Run home this instant and fetch me a pair of gloves and a fan!
Who in the world is Mary Ann?

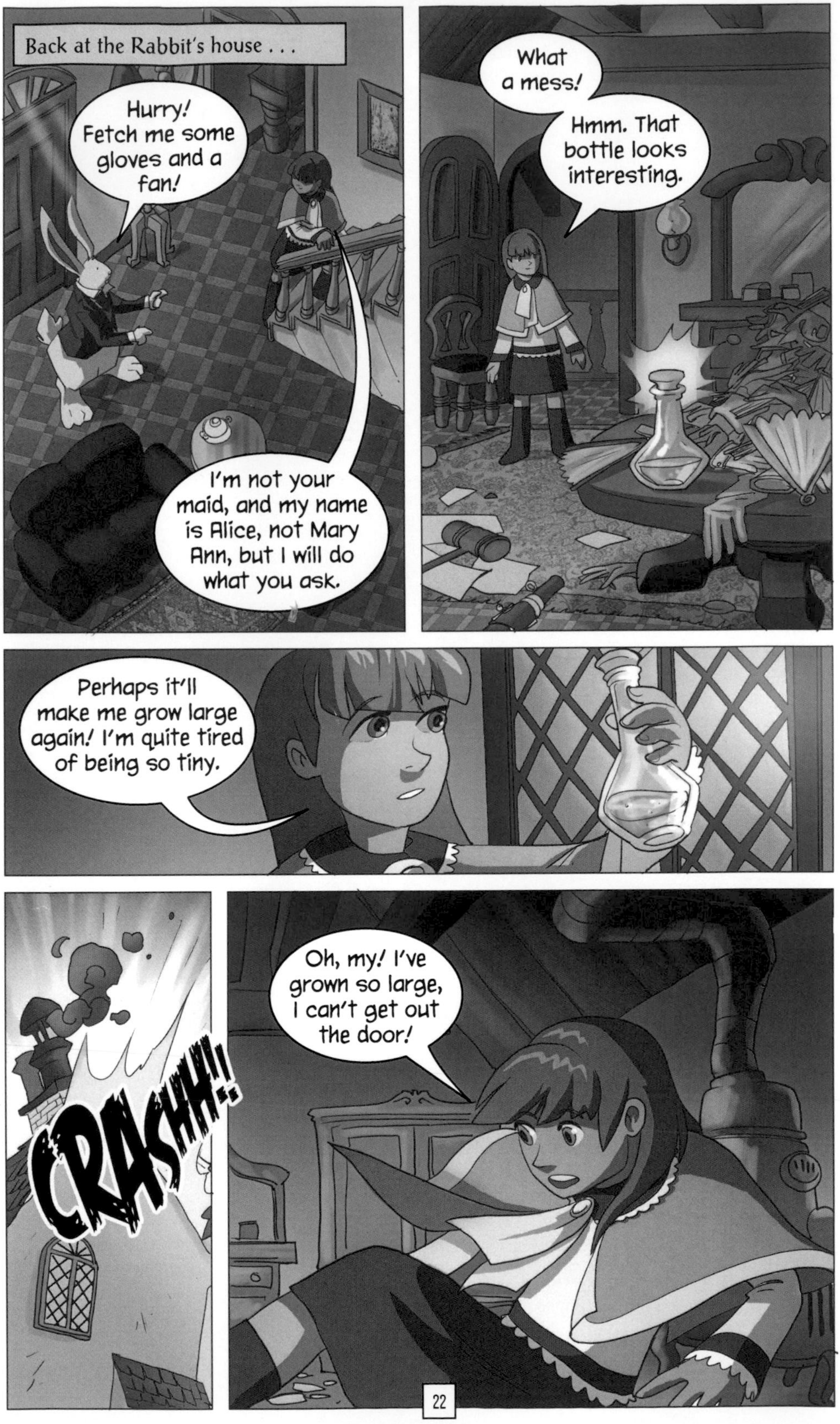
Back at the Rabbit's house . . .
Hurry! Fetch me some gloves and a fan!
I'm not your maid, and my name is Alice, not Mary Ann, but I will do what you ask.
What a mess!
Hmm. That bottle looks interesting.
Perhaps it'll make me grow large again! I'm quite tired of being so tiny.
CRASHH!!
Oh, my! I've grown so large, I can't get out the door!

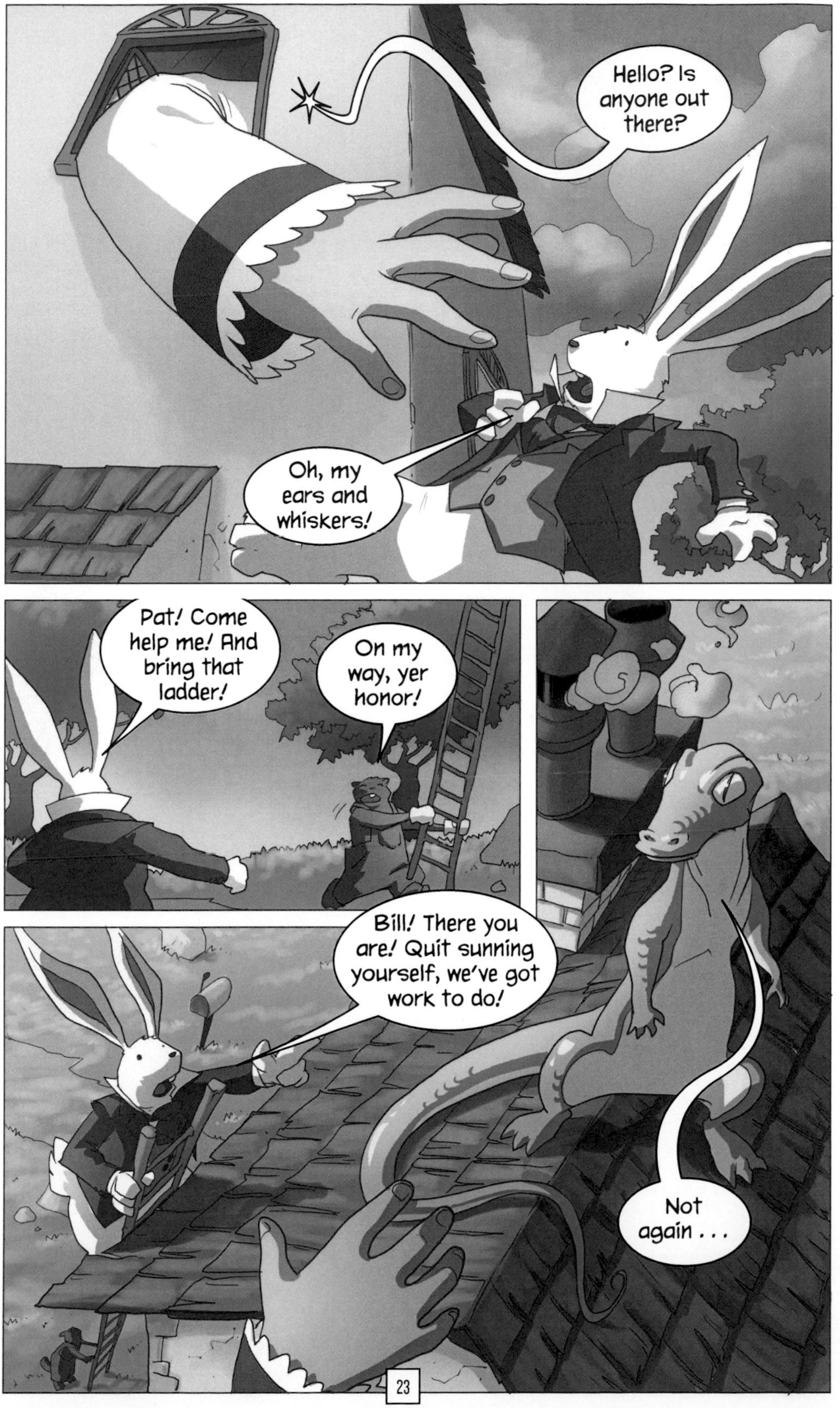

Hello? Is anyone out there?
Oh, my ears and whiskers!
Pat! Come help me! And bring that ladder!
On my way, yer honor!
Bill! There you are! Quit sunning yourself, we've got work to do!
Not again . . .

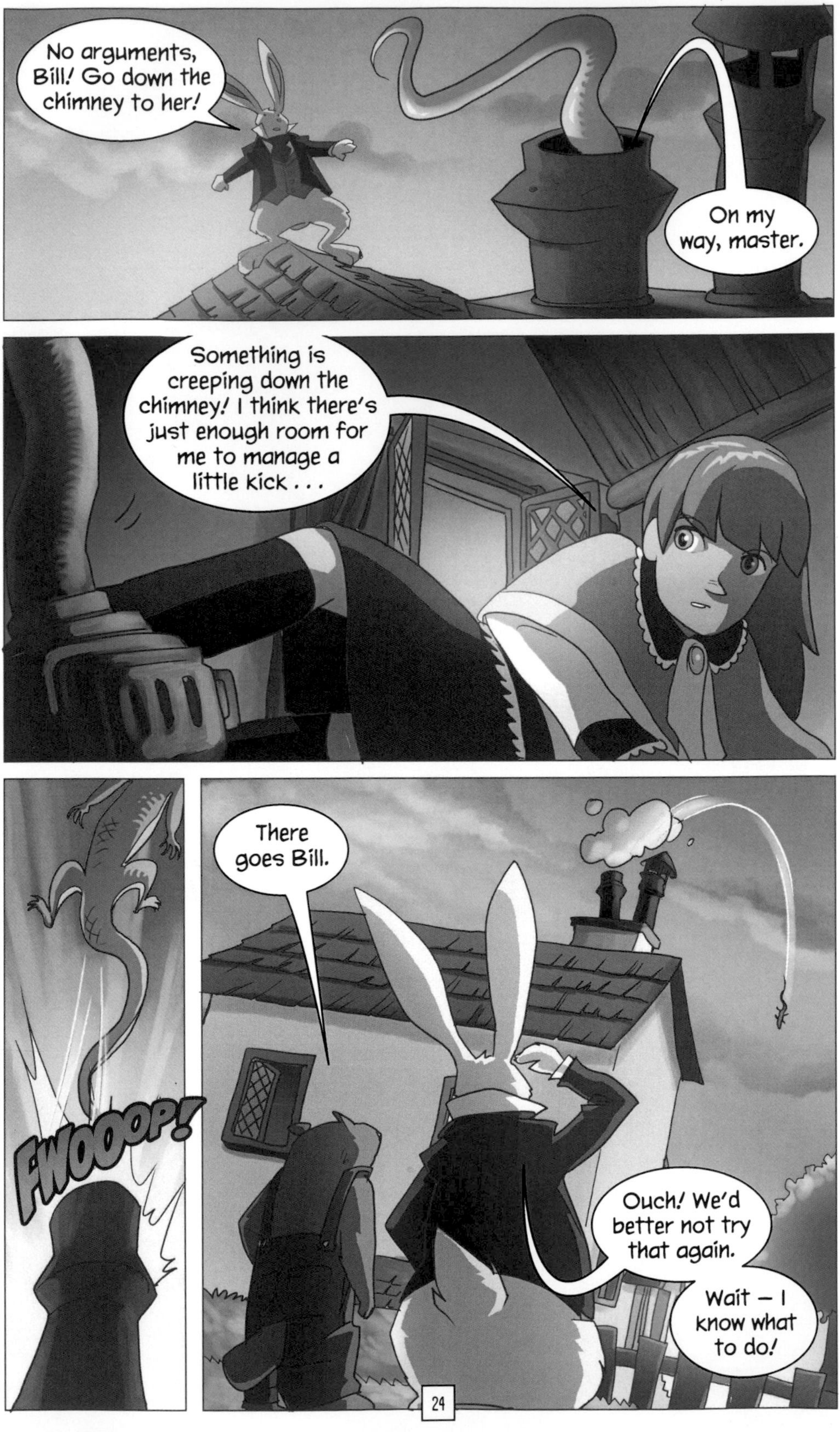
No arguments, Bill! Go down the chimney to her!
On my way, master.
Something is creeping down the chimney! I think there's just enough room for me to manage a little kick . . .
FWOOOP!
There goes Bill.
Ouch! We'd better not try that again.
Wait — I know what to do!

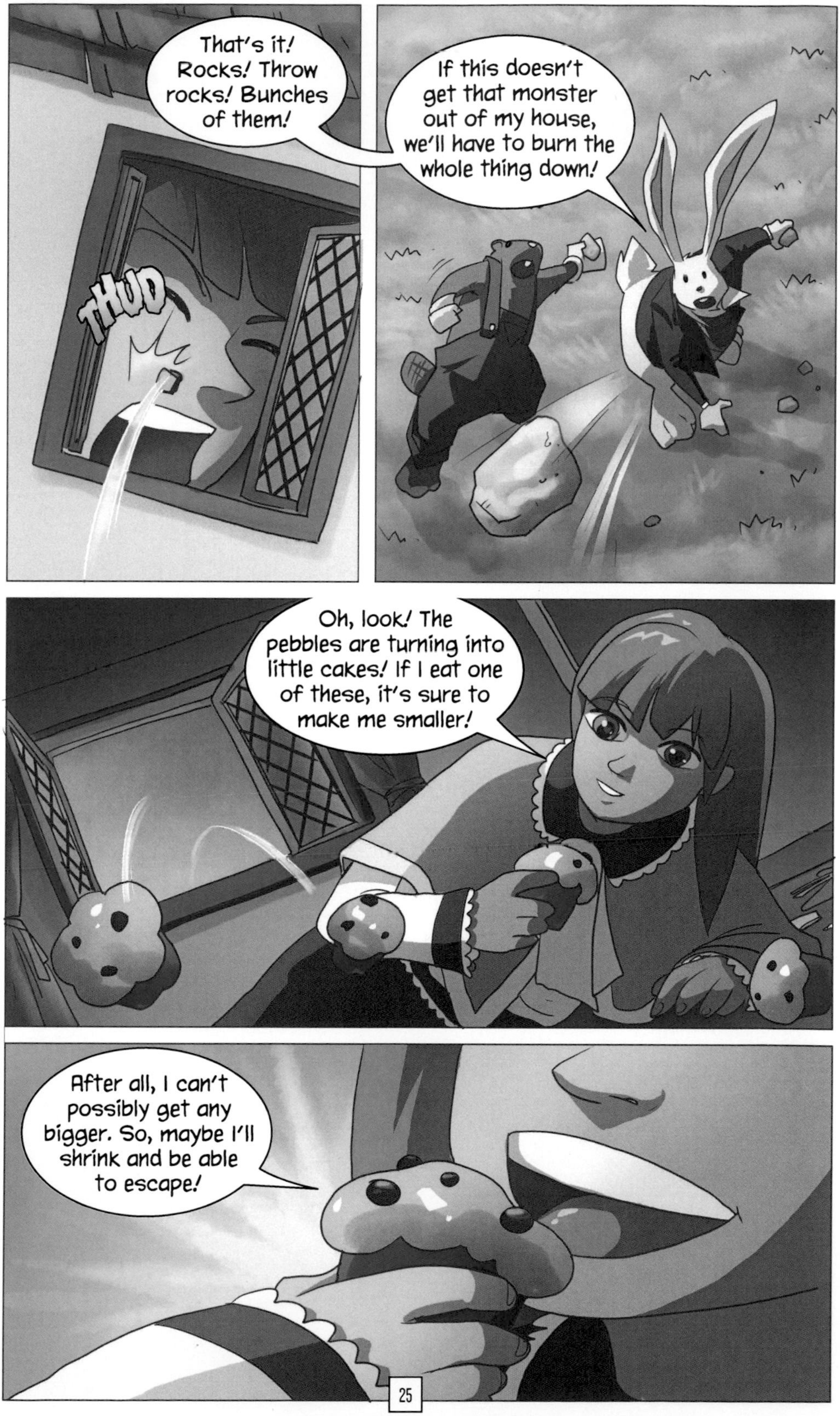
THUD
That's it! Rocks! Throw rocks! Bunches of them!
If this doesn't get that monster out of my house, we'll have to burn the whole thing down!
Oh, look! The pebbles are turning into little cakes! If I eat one of these, it's sure to make me smaller!
After all, I can't possibly get any bigger. So, maybe I'll shrink and be able to escape!

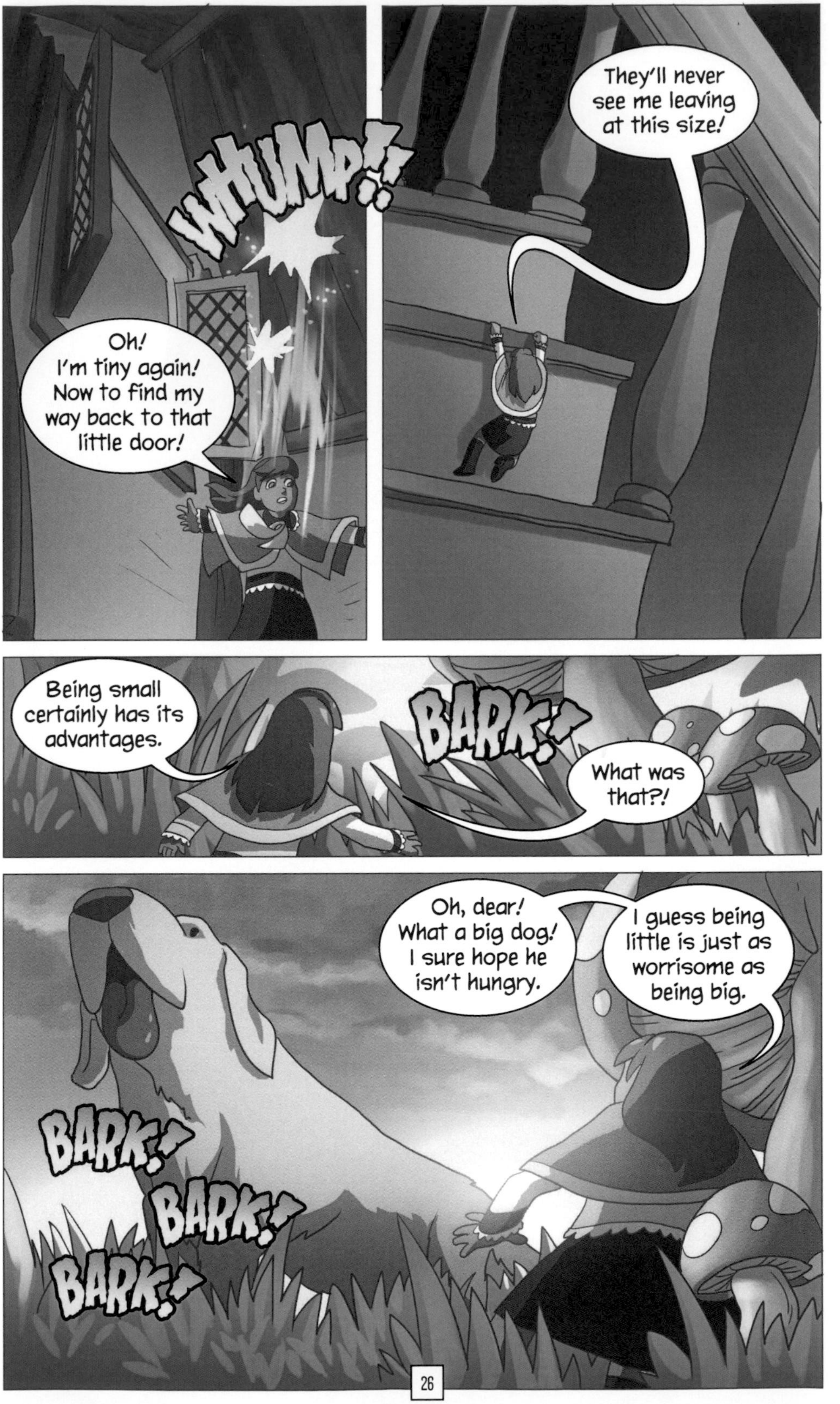
WHUMP!!
Oh! I'm tiny again! Now to find my way back to that little door!
They'll never see me leaving at this size!
Being small certainly has its advantages.
BARK!
What was that?!
Oh, dear! What a big dog! I sure hope he isn't hungry.
I guess being little is just as worrisome as being big.
BARK!
BARK!
BARK!

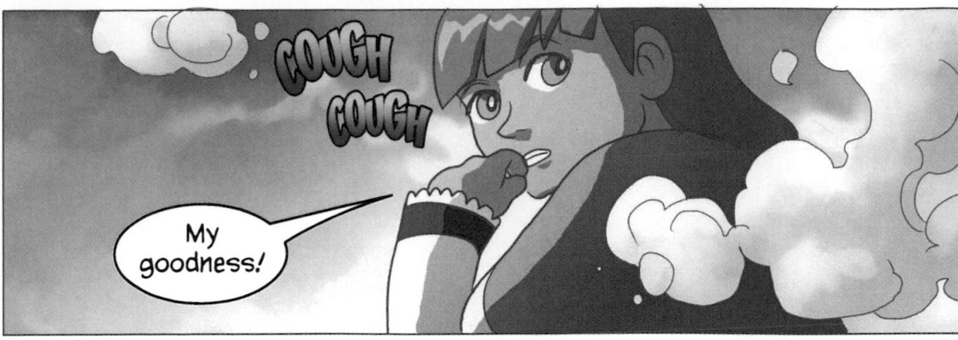
COUGH
COUGH
My goodness!

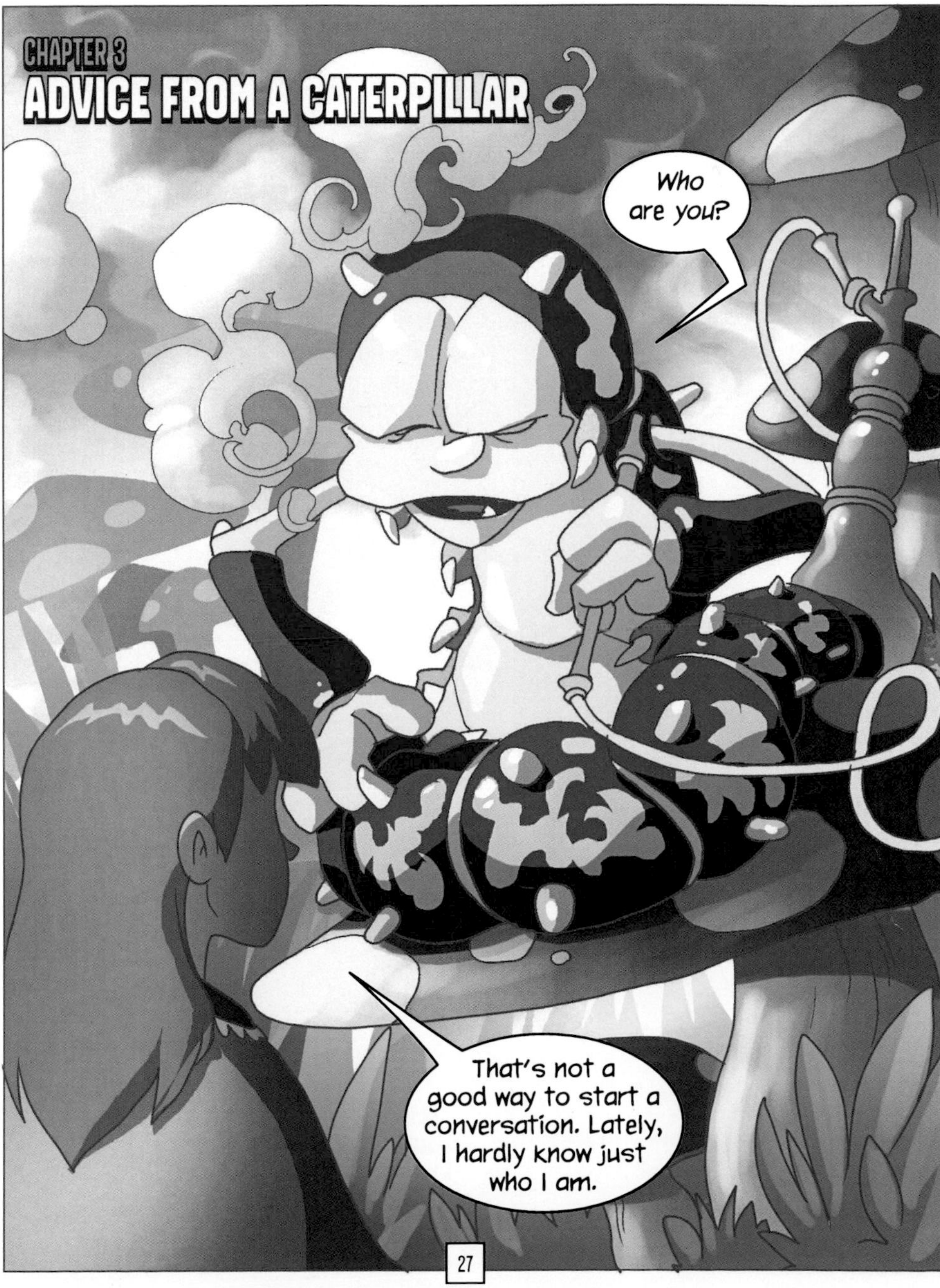
CHAPTER 3
ADVICE FROM A CATERPILLAR
Who are you?
That's not a good way to start a conversation. Lately, I hardly know just who I am.

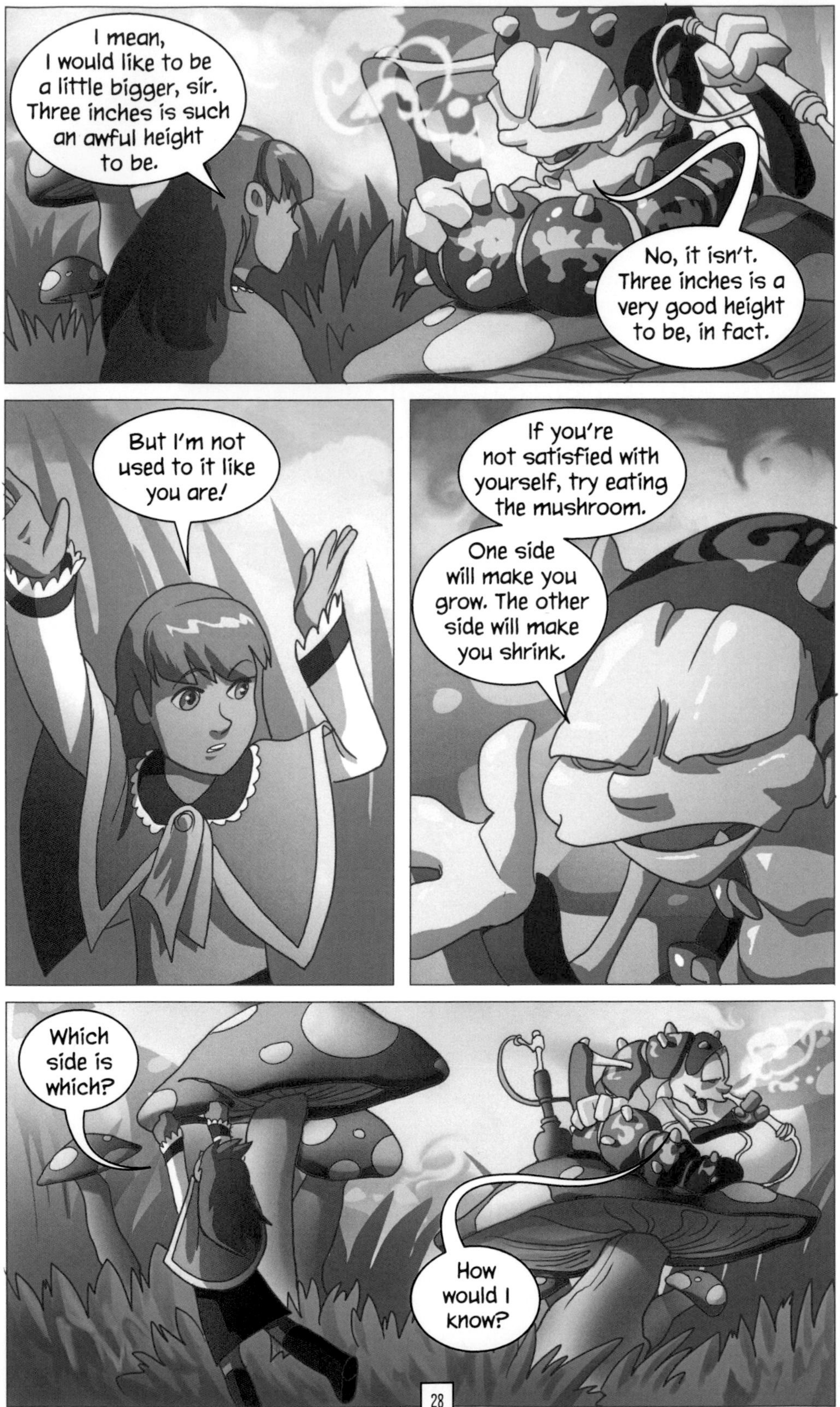
I mean, I would like to be a little bigger, sir. Three inches is such an awful height to be.
No, it isn't. Three inches is a very good height to be, in fact.
But I'm not used to it like you are!
If you're not satisfied with yourself, try eating the mushroom.
One side will make you grow. The other side will make you shrink.
Which side is which?
How would I know?

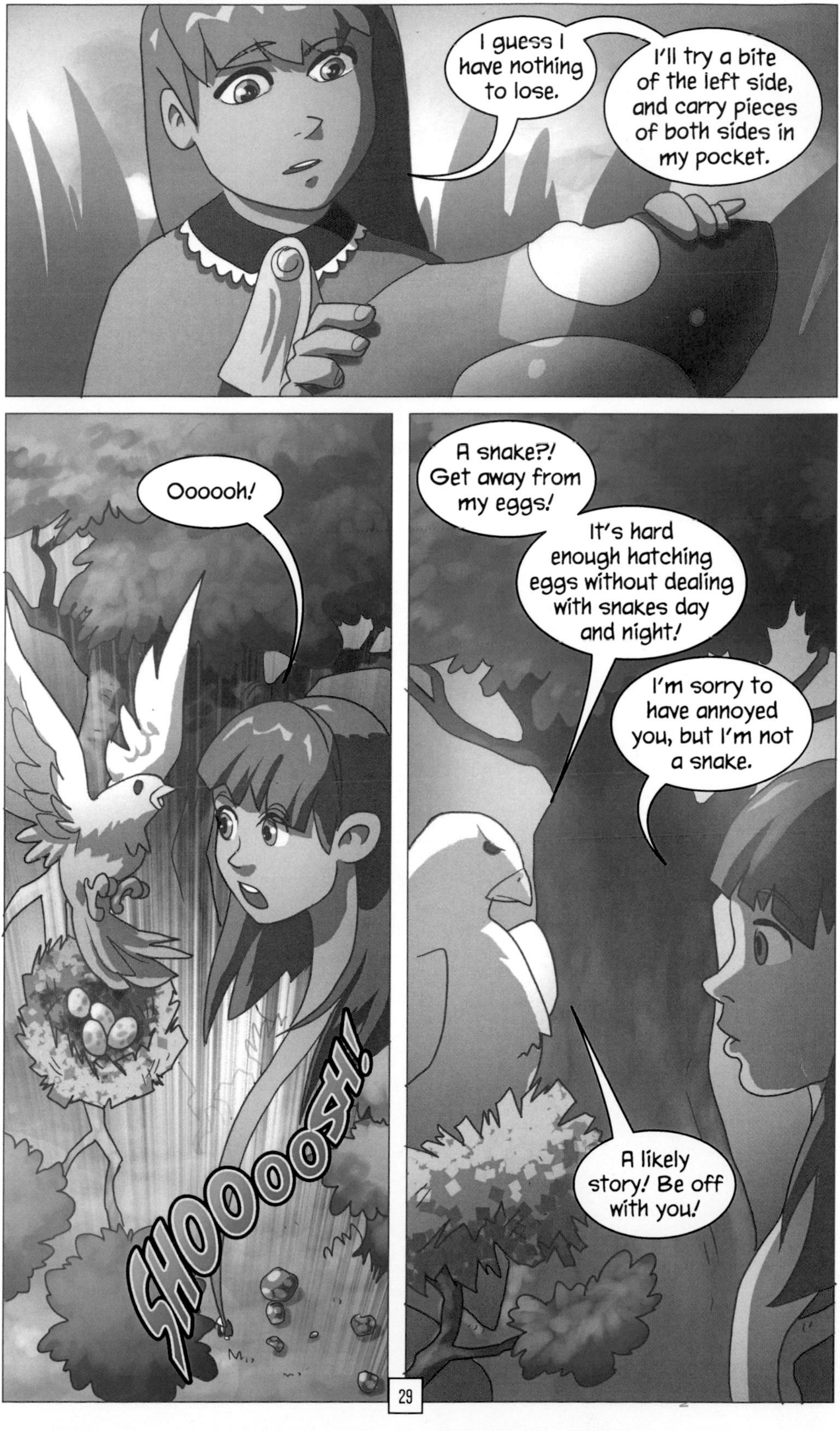
I guess I have nothing to lose.
I'll try a bite of the left side, and carry pieces of both sides in my pocket.
Oooooh!
SHOOOOOSH!
A snake?! Get away from my eggs!
It's hard enough hatching eggs without dealing with snakes day and night!
I'm sorry to have annoyed you, but I'm not a snake.
A likely story! Be off with you!

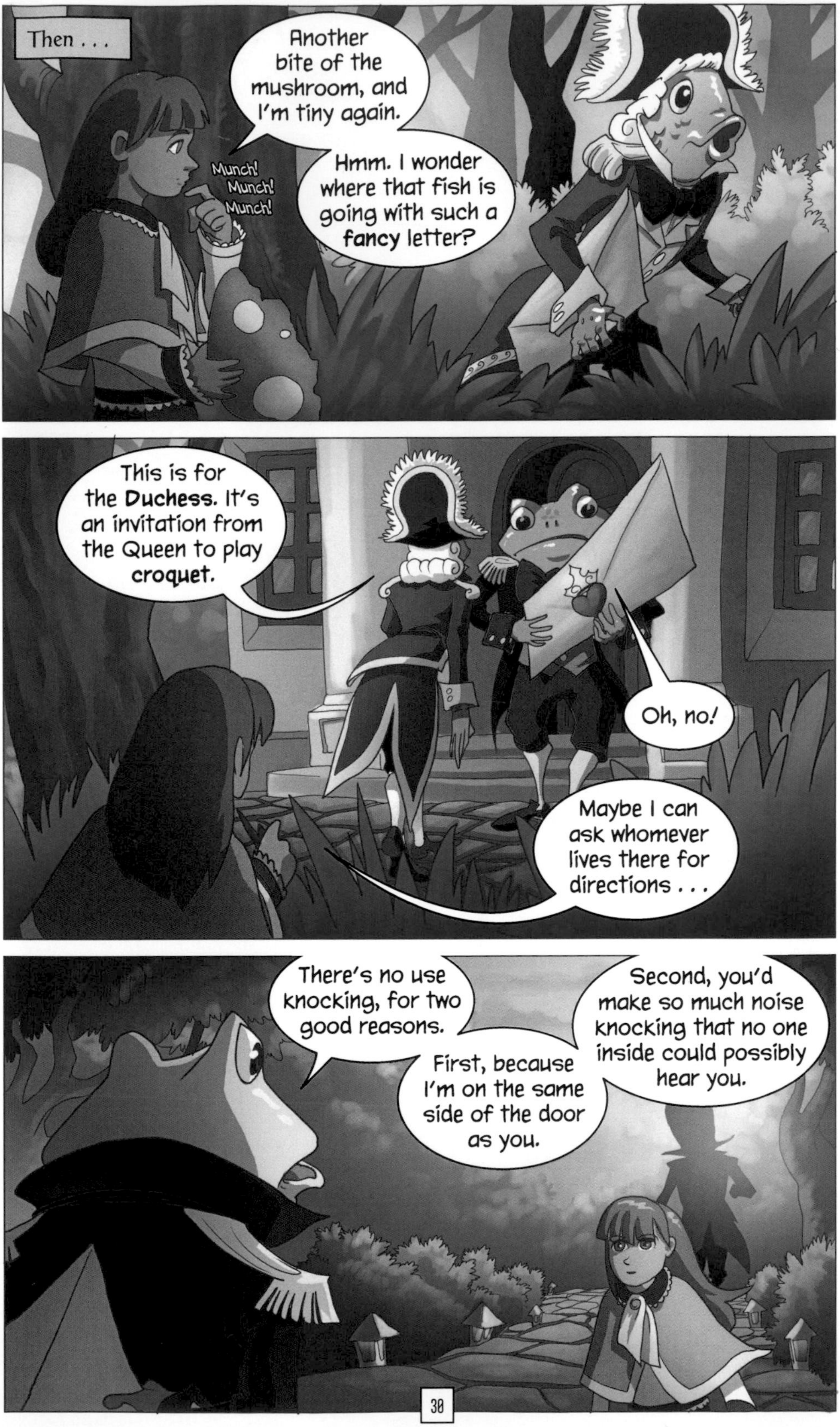
Then . . .
Another bite of the mushroom, and I'm tiny again.
Munch! Munch! Munch!
Hmm. I wonder where that fish is going with such a **fancy** letter?
This is for the **Duchess**. It's an invitation from the Queen to play **croquet**.
Oh, no!
Maybe I can ask whomever lives there for directions . . .
There's no use knocking, for two good reasons.
First, because I'm on the same side of the door as you.
Second, you'd make so much noise knocking that no one inside could possibly hear you.

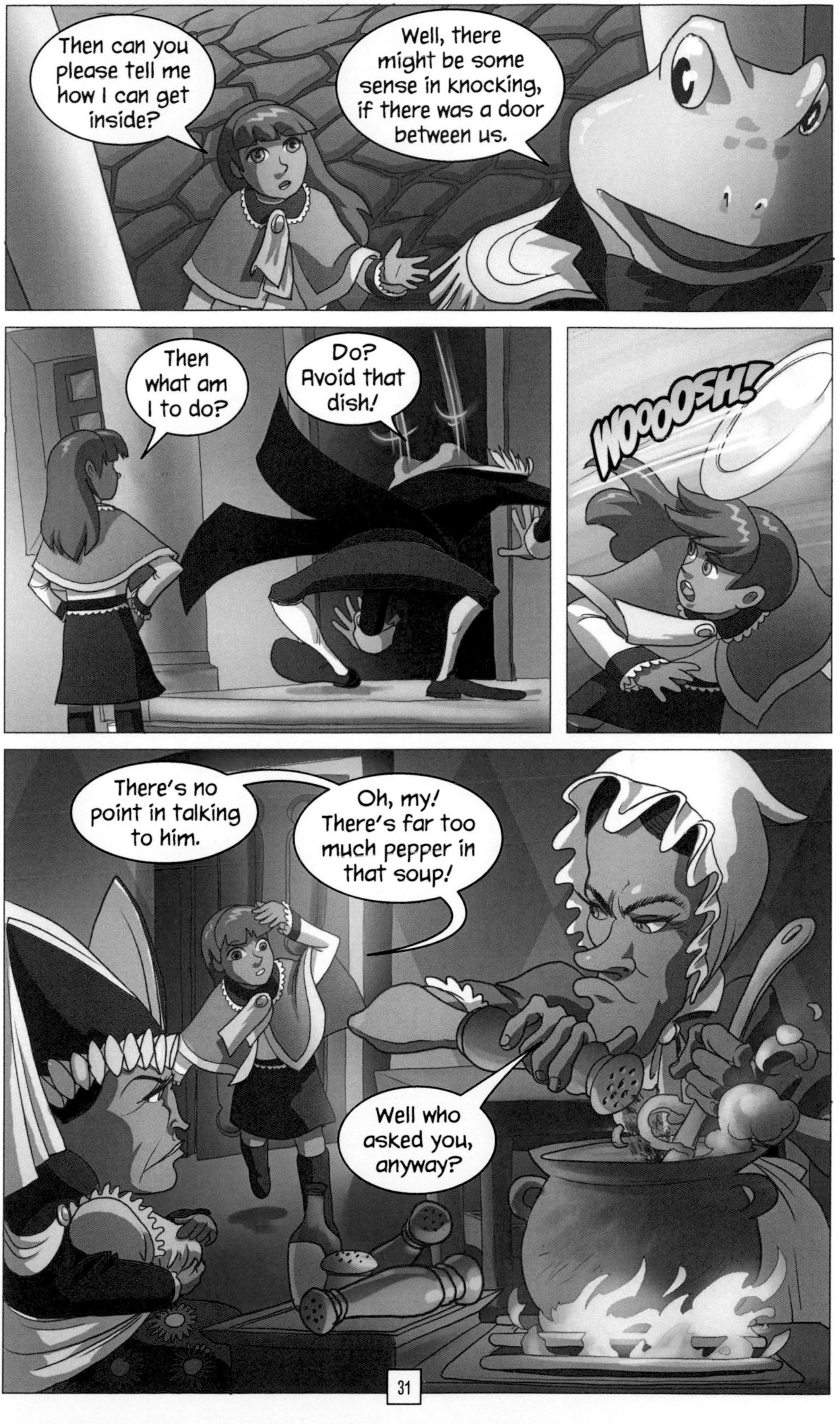
Then can you please tell me how I can get inside?
Well, there might be some sense in knocking, if there was a door between us.
Then what am I to do?
Do? Avoid that dish!
WOOOOSH!
There's no point in talking to him.
Oh, my! There's far too much pepper in that soup!
Well who asked you, anyway?

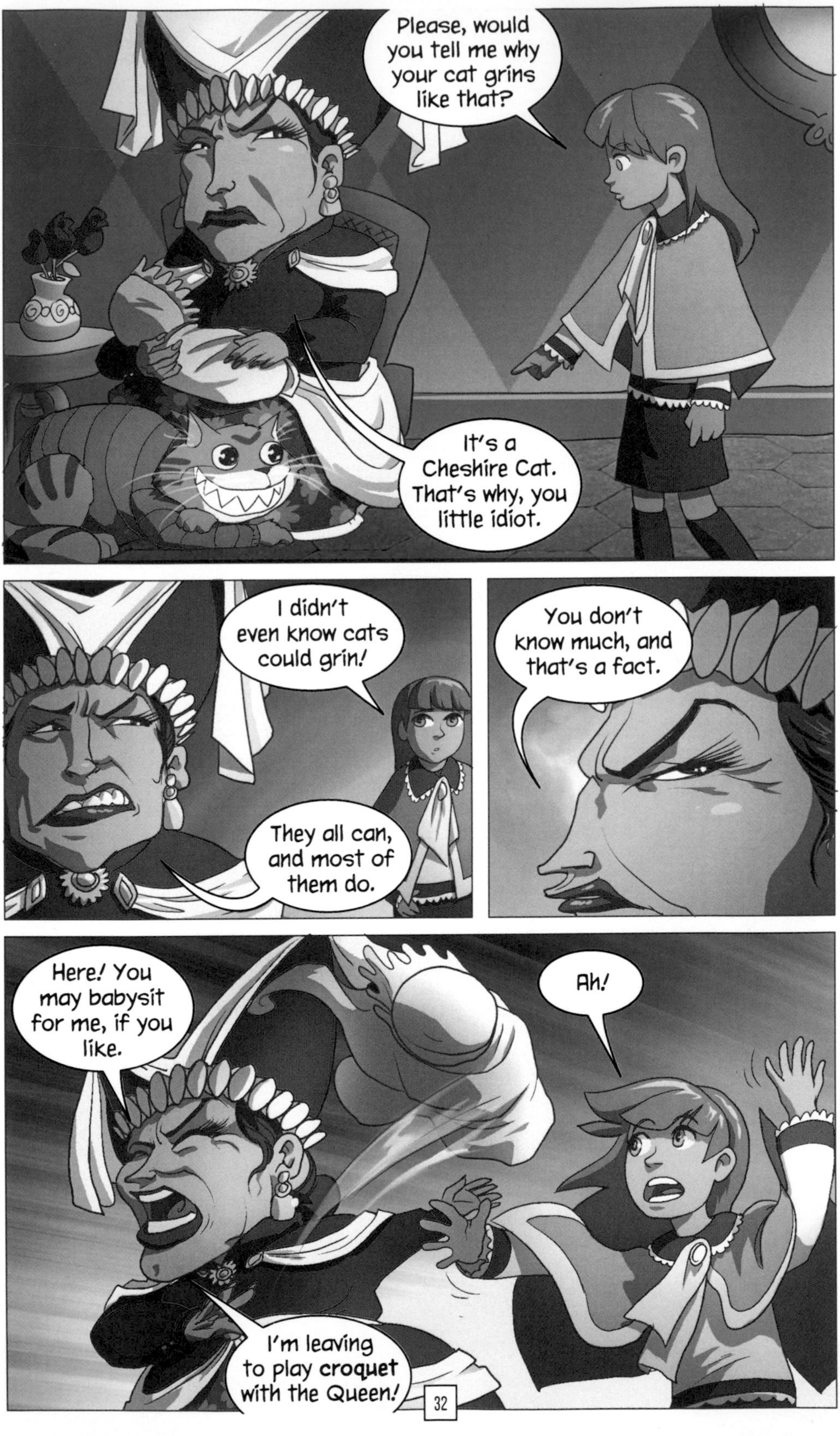

Please, would you tell me why your cat grins like that?
It's a Cheshire Cat. That's why, you little idiot.
I didn't even know cats could grin!
They all can, and most of them do.
You don't know much, and that's a fact.
Here! You may babysit for me, if you like.
Ah!
I'm leaving to play **croquet** with the Queen!

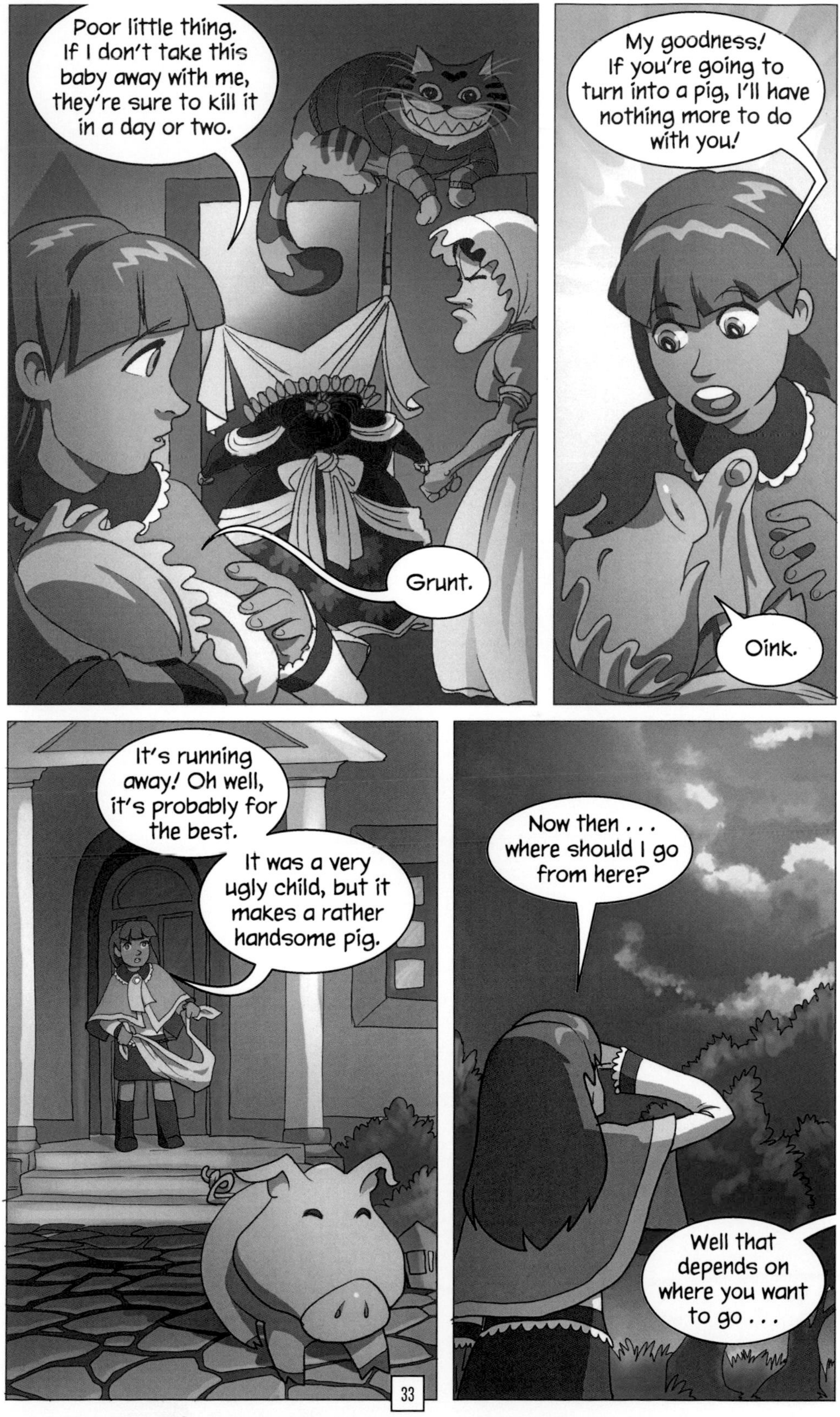
Poor little thing. If I don't take this baby away with me, they're sure to kill it in a day or two.
Grunt.
My goodness! If you're going to turn into a pig, I'll have nothing more to do with you!
Oink.
It's running away! Oh well, it's probably for the best.
It was a very ugly child, but it makes a rather handsome pig.
Now then . . . where should I go from here?
Well that depends on where you want to go . . .

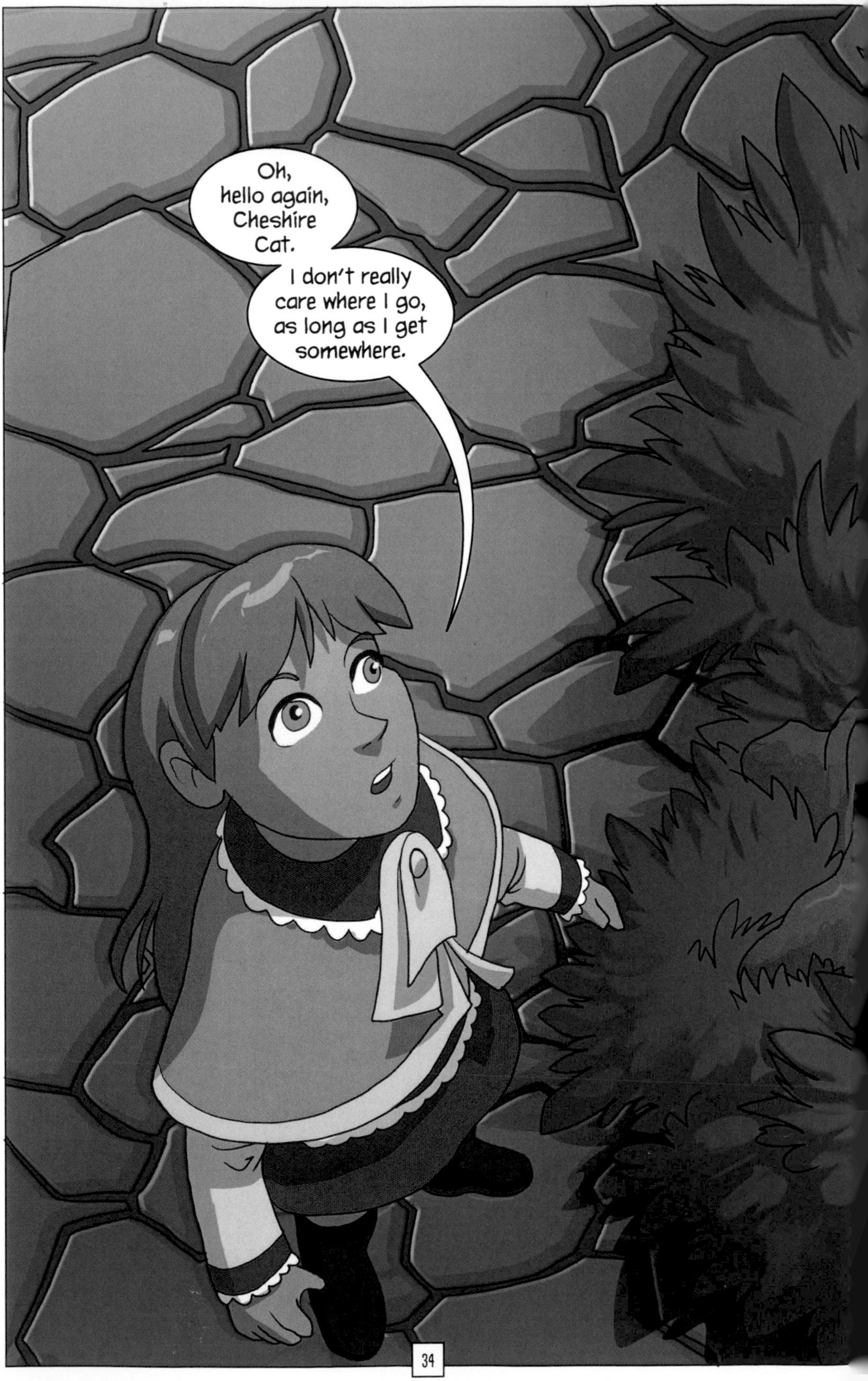
Oh, hello again, Cheshire Cat.
I don't really care where I go, as long as I get somewhere.

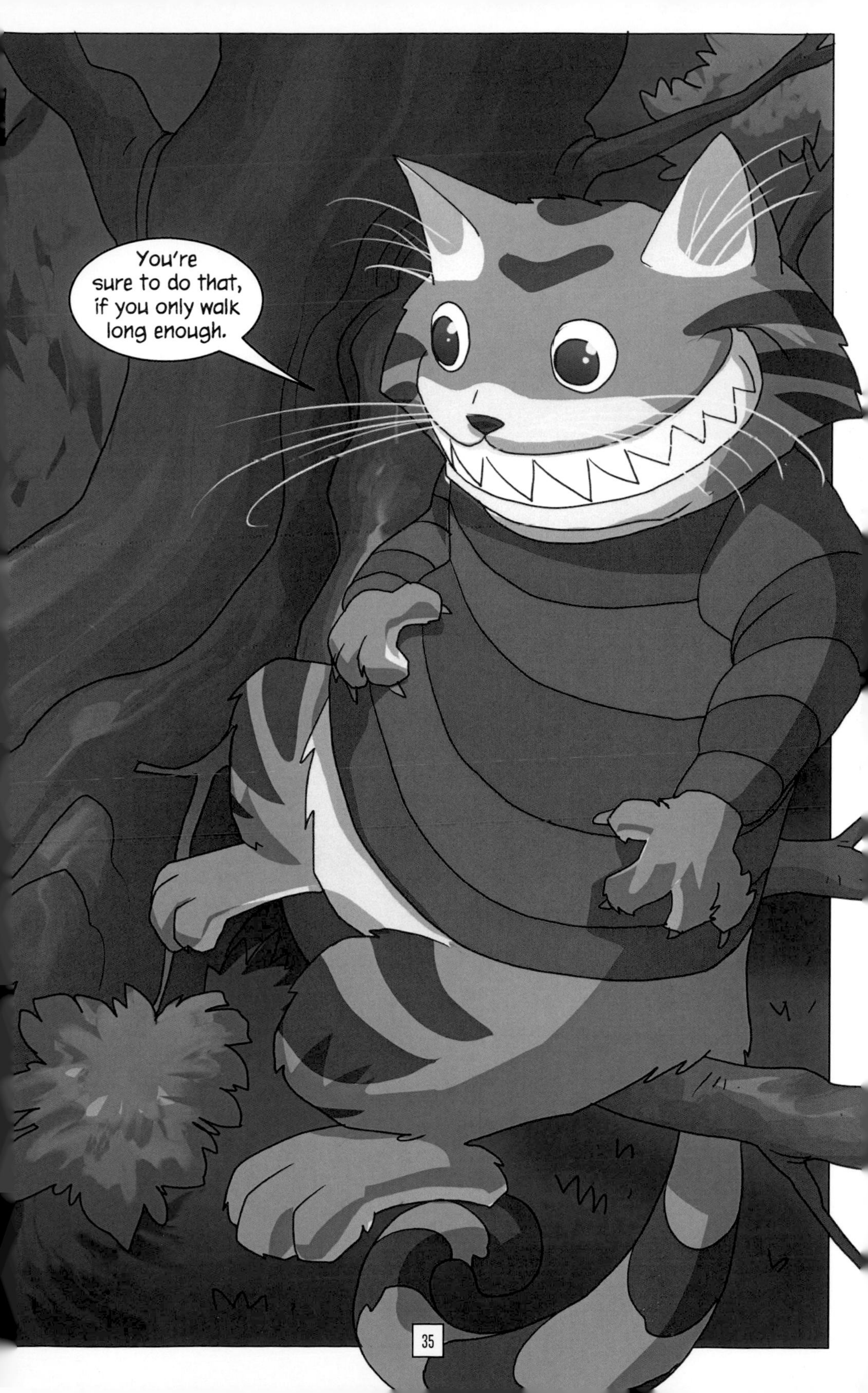
You're sure to do that, if you only walk long enough.

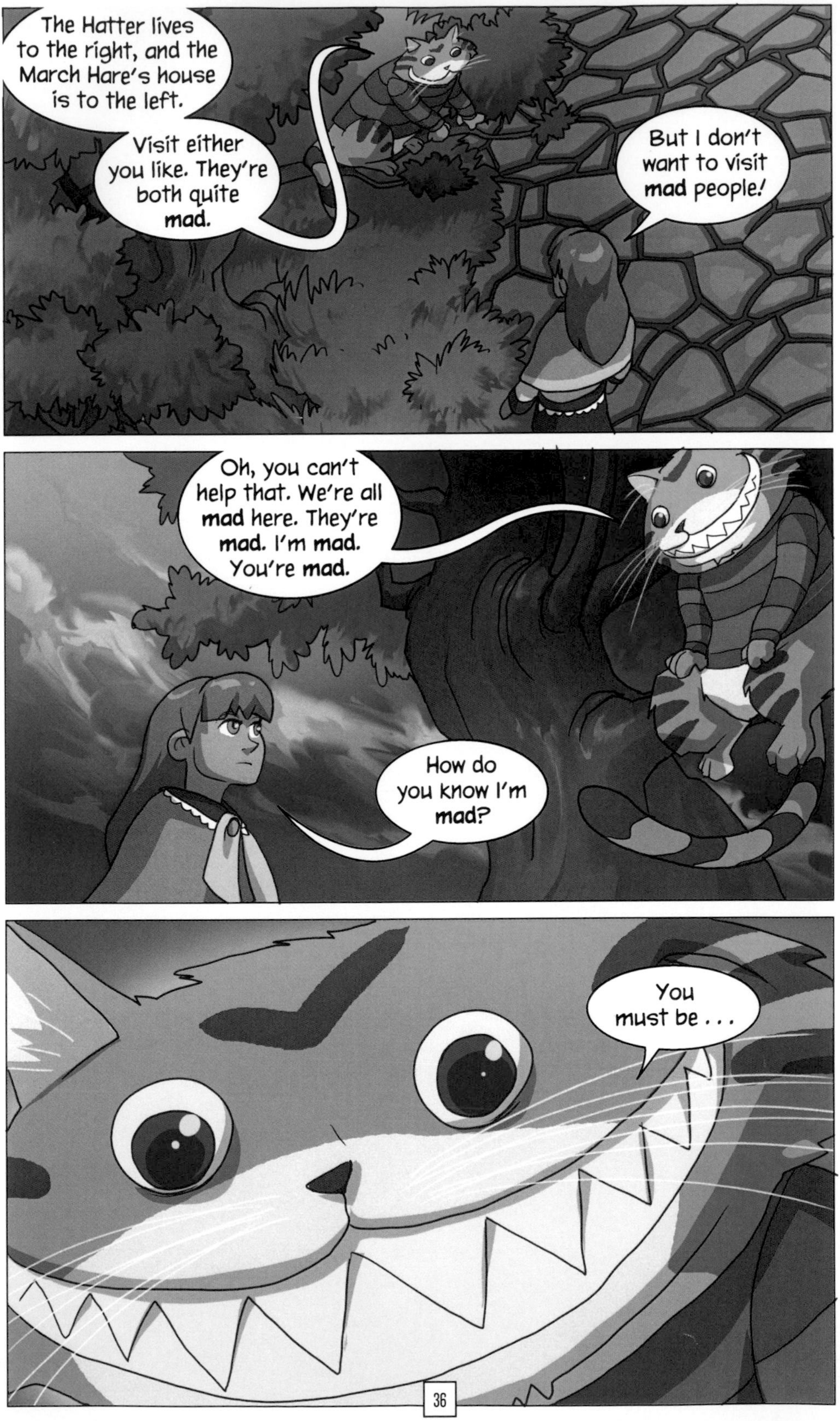
The Hatter lives to the right, and the March Hare's house is to the left.
Visit either you like. They're both quite **mad**.
But I don't want to visit **mad** people!
Oh, you can't help that. We're all **mad** here. They're **mad**. I'm **mad**. You're **mad**.
How do you know I'm **mad**?
You must be . . .

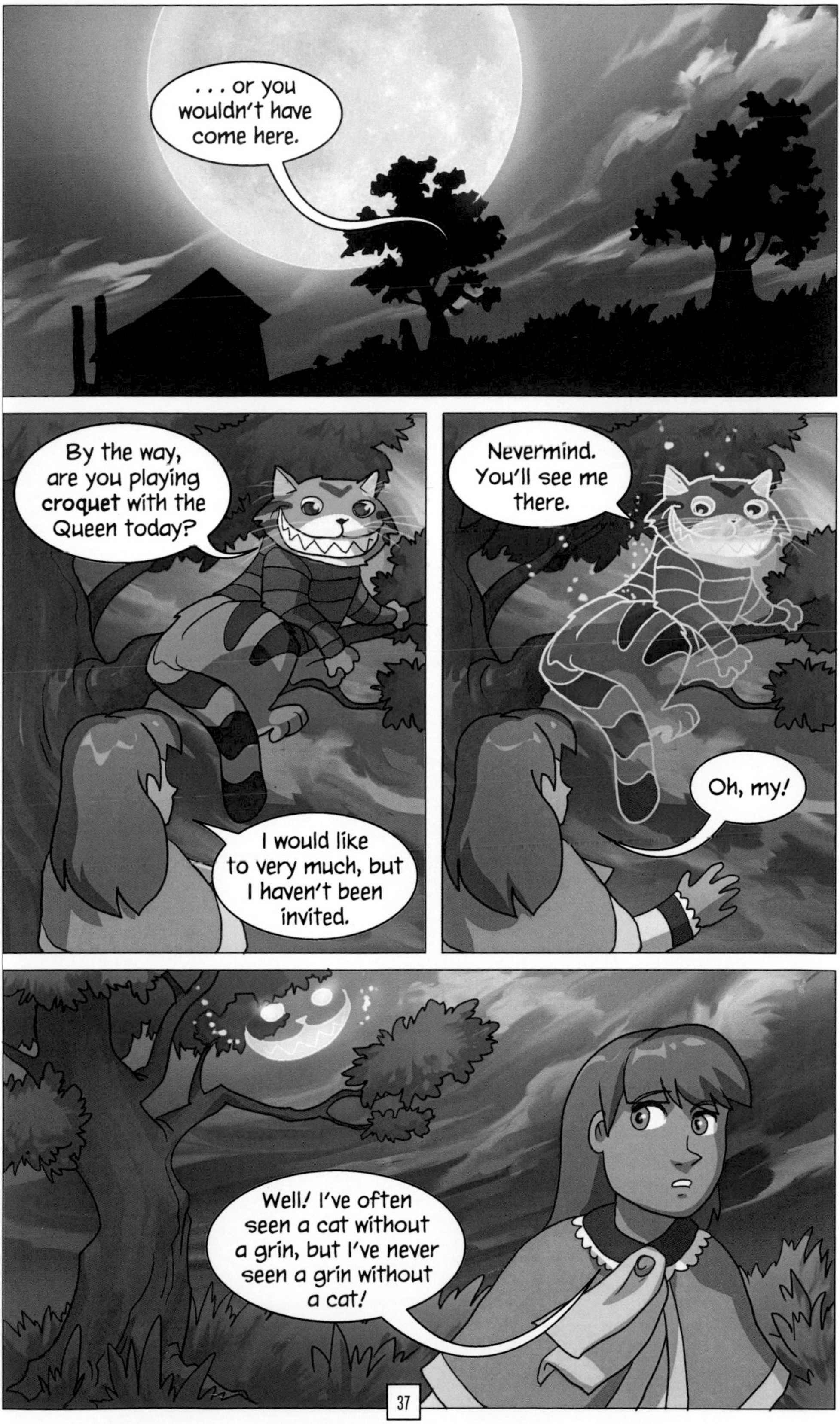
. . . or you wouldn't have come here.
By the way, are you playing **croquet** with the Queen today?
I would like to very much, but I haven't been invited.
Nevermind. You'll see me there.
Oh, my!
Well! I've often seen a cat without a grin, but I've never seen a grin without a cat!

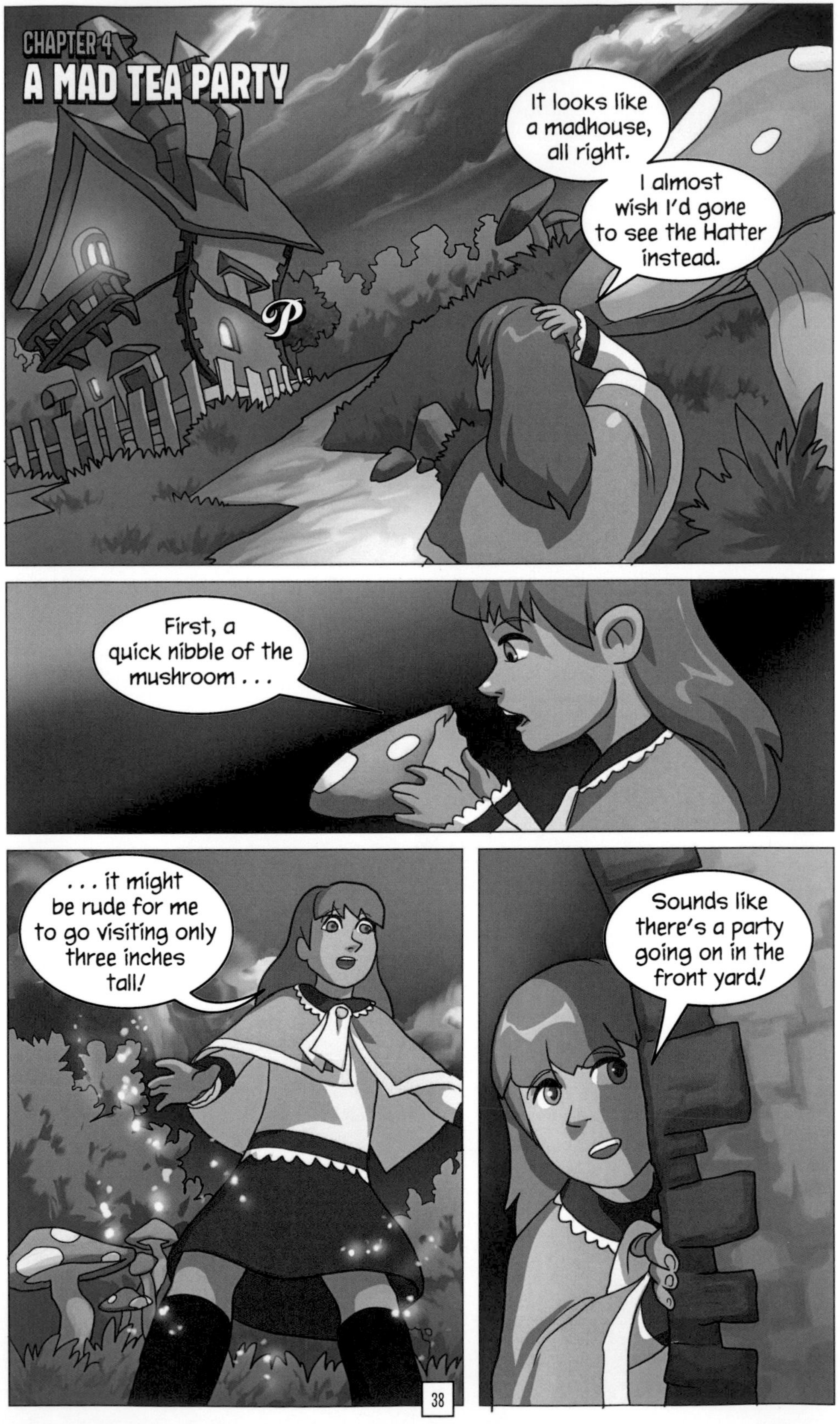
CHAPTER 4
A MAD TEA PARTY
It looks like a madhouse, all right.
I almost wish I'd gone to see the Hatter instead.
First, a quick nibble of the mushroom . . .
. . . it might be rude for me to go visiting only three inches tall!
Sounds like there's a party going on in the front yard!

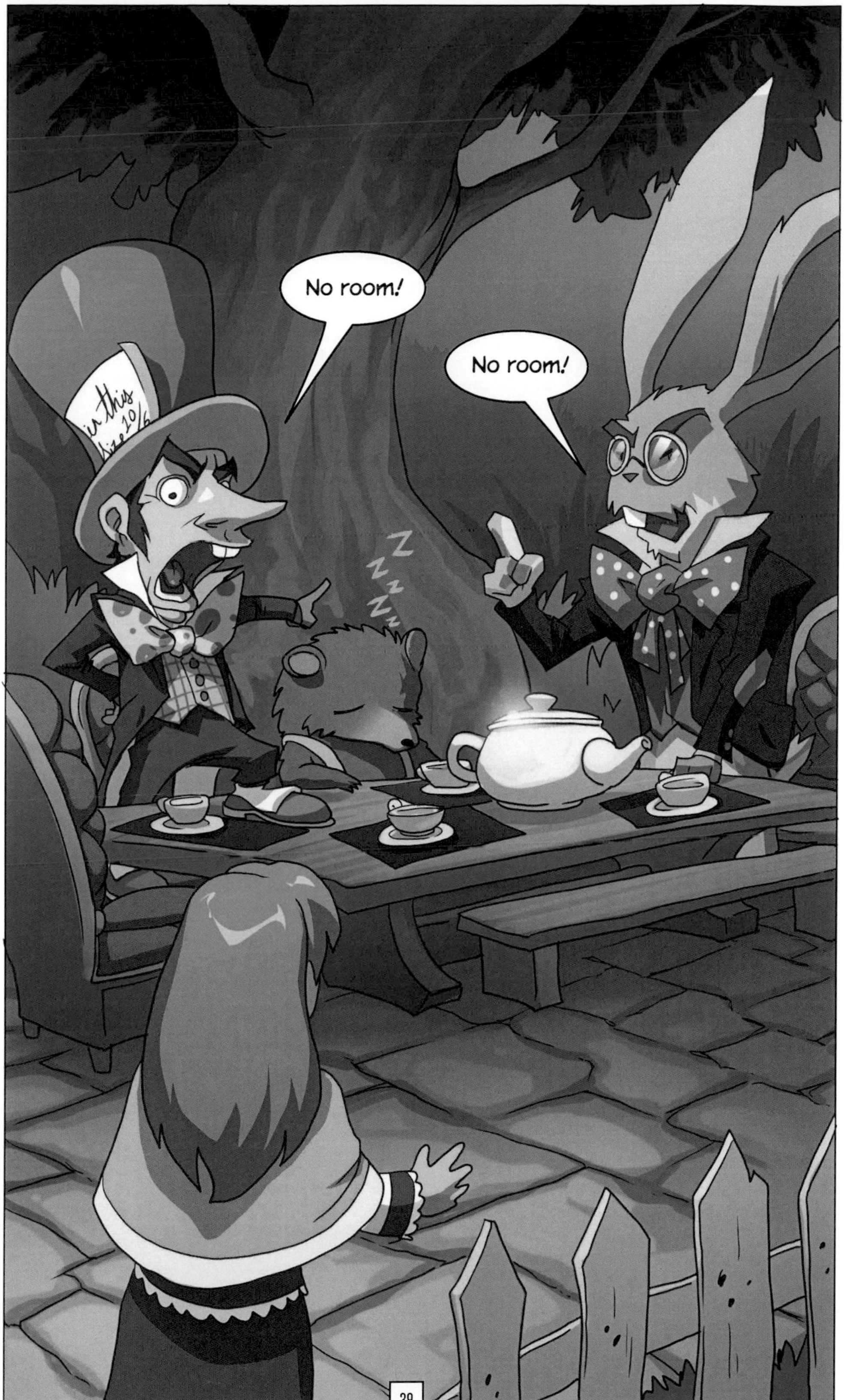
No room!
No room!

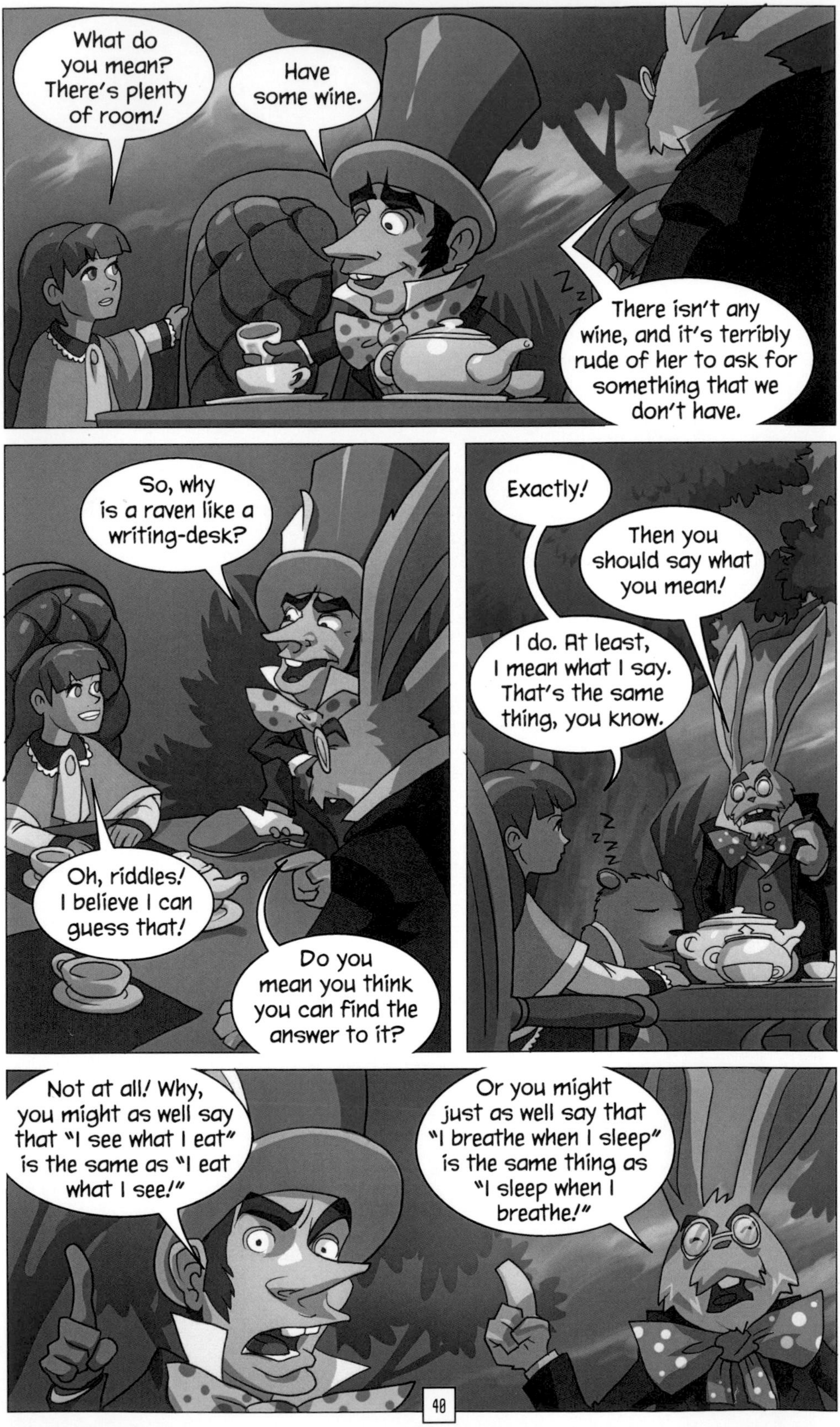

What do you mean? There's plenty of room!
Have some wine.
There isn't any wine, and it's terribly rude of her to ask for something that we don't have.
So, why is a raven like a writing-desk?
Oh, riddles! I believe I can guess that!
Do you mean you think you can find the answer to it?
Exactly!
Then you should say what you mean!
I do. At least, I mean what I say. That's the same thing, you know.
Not at all! Why, you might as well say that "I see what I eat" is the same as "I eat what I see!"
Or you might just as well say that "I breathe when I sleep" is the same thing as "I sleep when I breathe!"

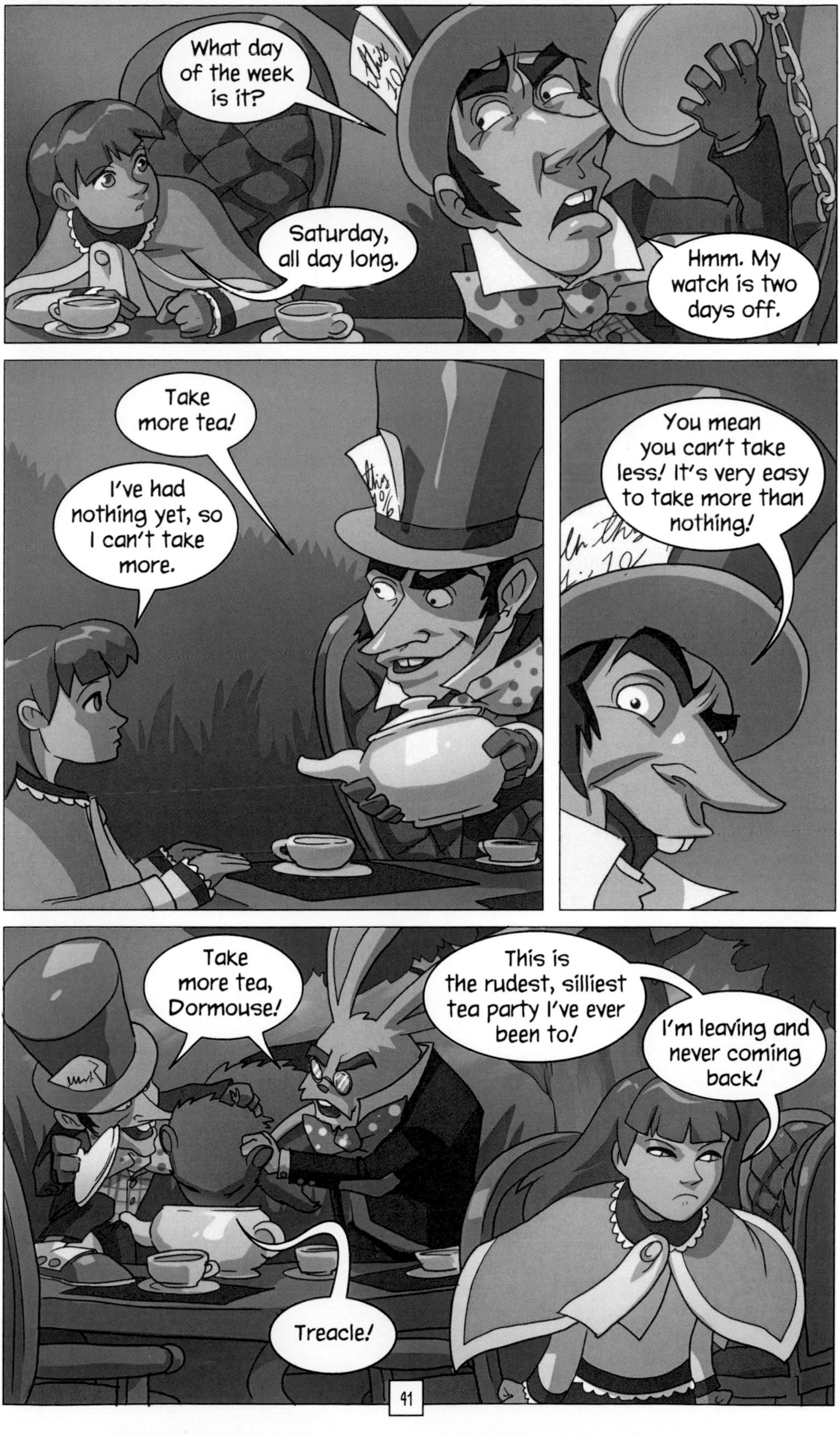
What day of the week is it?
Saturday, all day long.
Hmm. My watch is two days off.
Take more tea!
I've had nothing yet, so I can't take more.
You mean you can't take less! It's very easy to take more than nothing!
Take more tea, Dormouse!
Treacle!
This is the rudest, silliest tea party I've ever been to!
I'm leaving and never coming back!

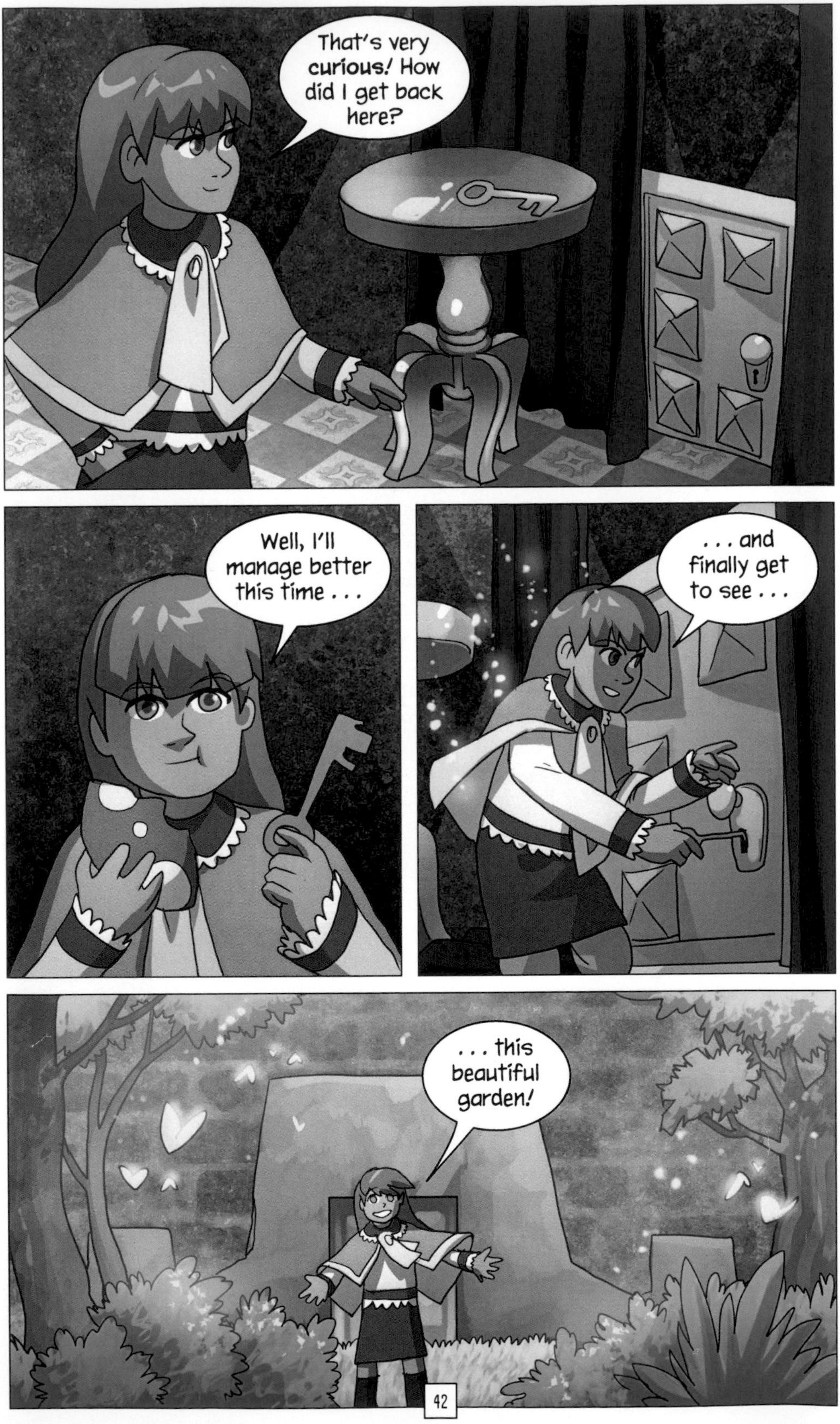
That's very curious! How did I get back here?
Well, I'll manage better this time . . .
. . . and finally get to see . . .
. . . this beautiful garden!

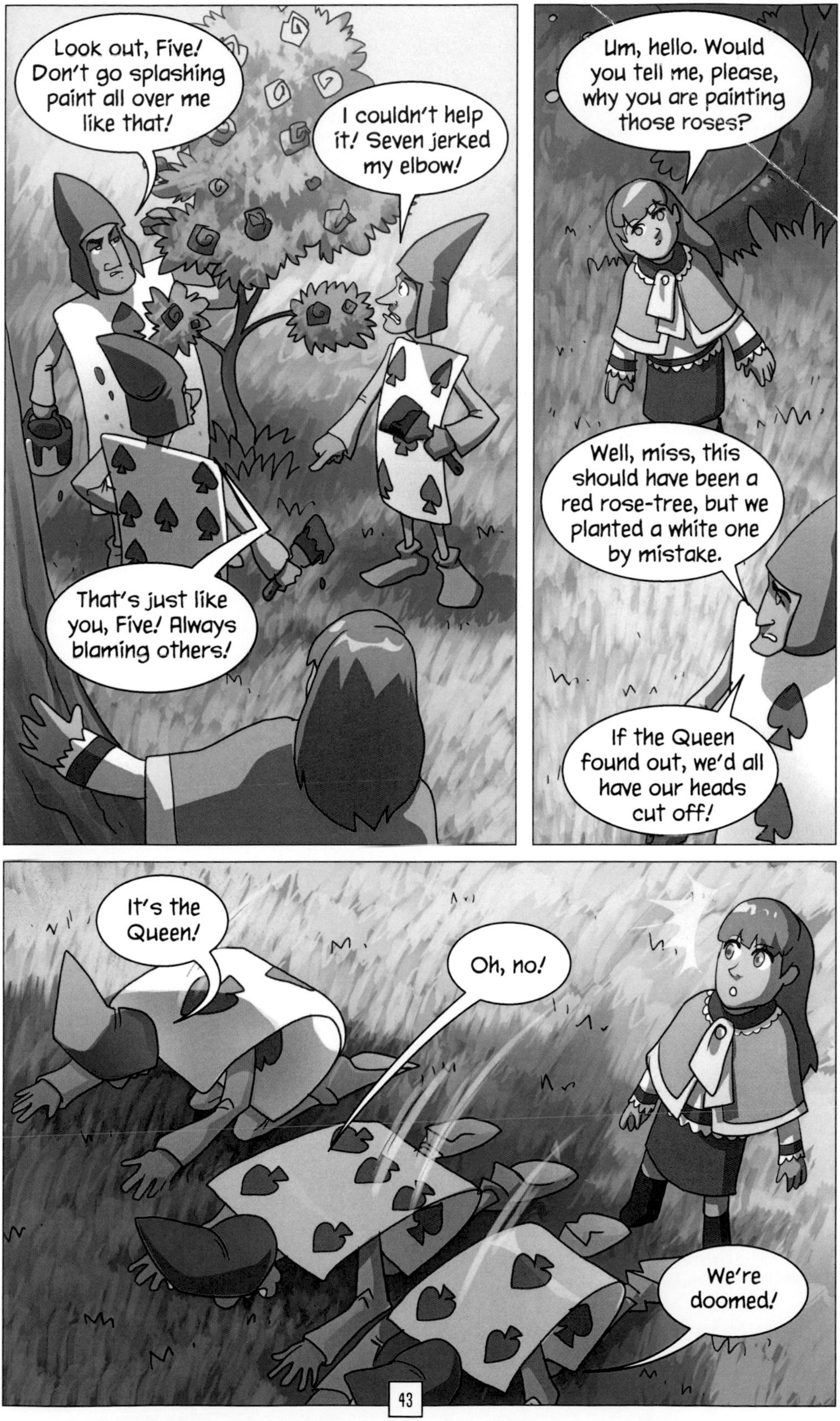
Look out, Five! Don't go splashing paint all over me like that!
I couldn't help it! Seven jerked my elbow!
That's just like you, Five! Always blaming others!
Um, hello. Would you tell me, please, why you are painting those roses?
Well, miss, this should have been a red rose-tree, but we planted a white one by mistake.
If the Queen found out, we'd all have our heads cut off!
It's the Queen!
Oh, no!
We're doomed!

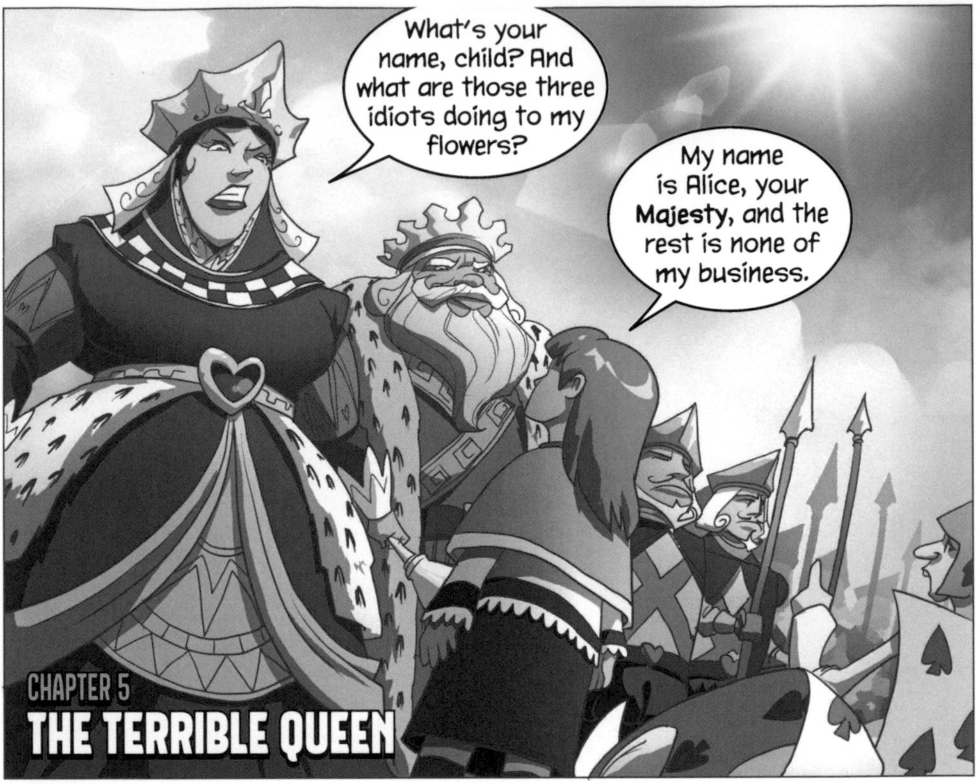
What's your name, child? And what are those three idiots doing to my flowers?
My name is Alice, your **Majesty**, and the rest is none of my business.
CHAPTER 5
THE TERRIBLE QUEEN

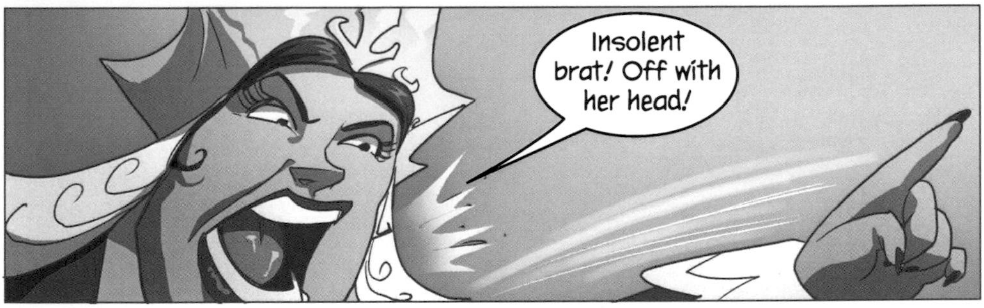
Insolent brat! Off with her head!

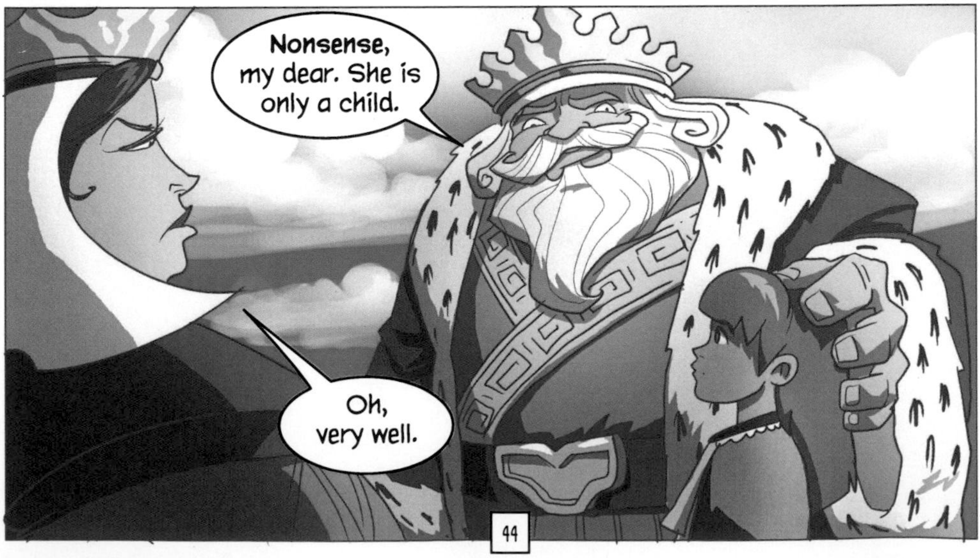
**Nonsense**, my dear. She is only a child.
Oh, very well.

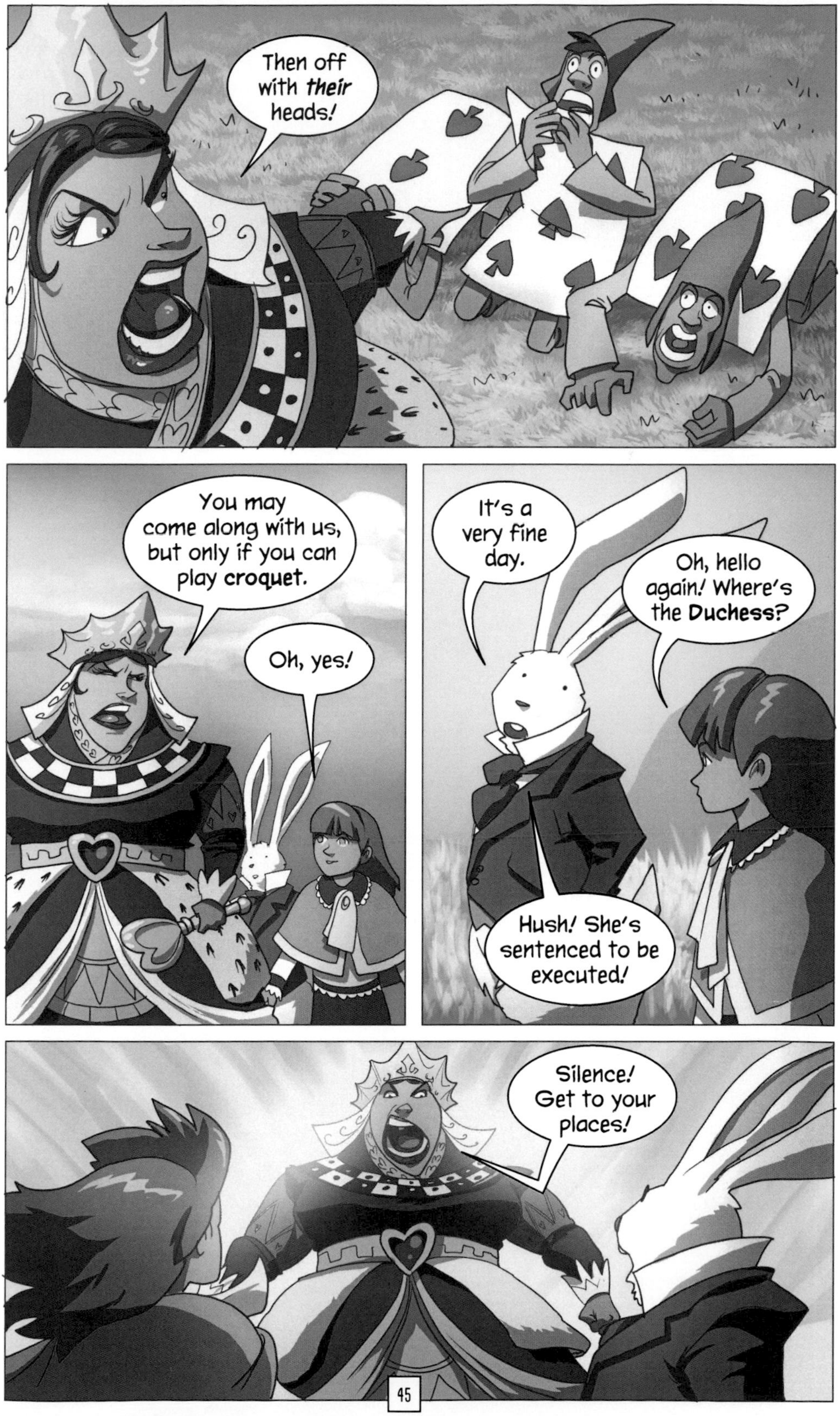
Then off with **their** heads!
You may come along with us, but only if you can play **croquet**.
Oh, yes!
It's a very fine day.
Oh, hello again! Where's the **Duchess**?
Hush! She's sentenced to be executed!
Silence! Get to your places!

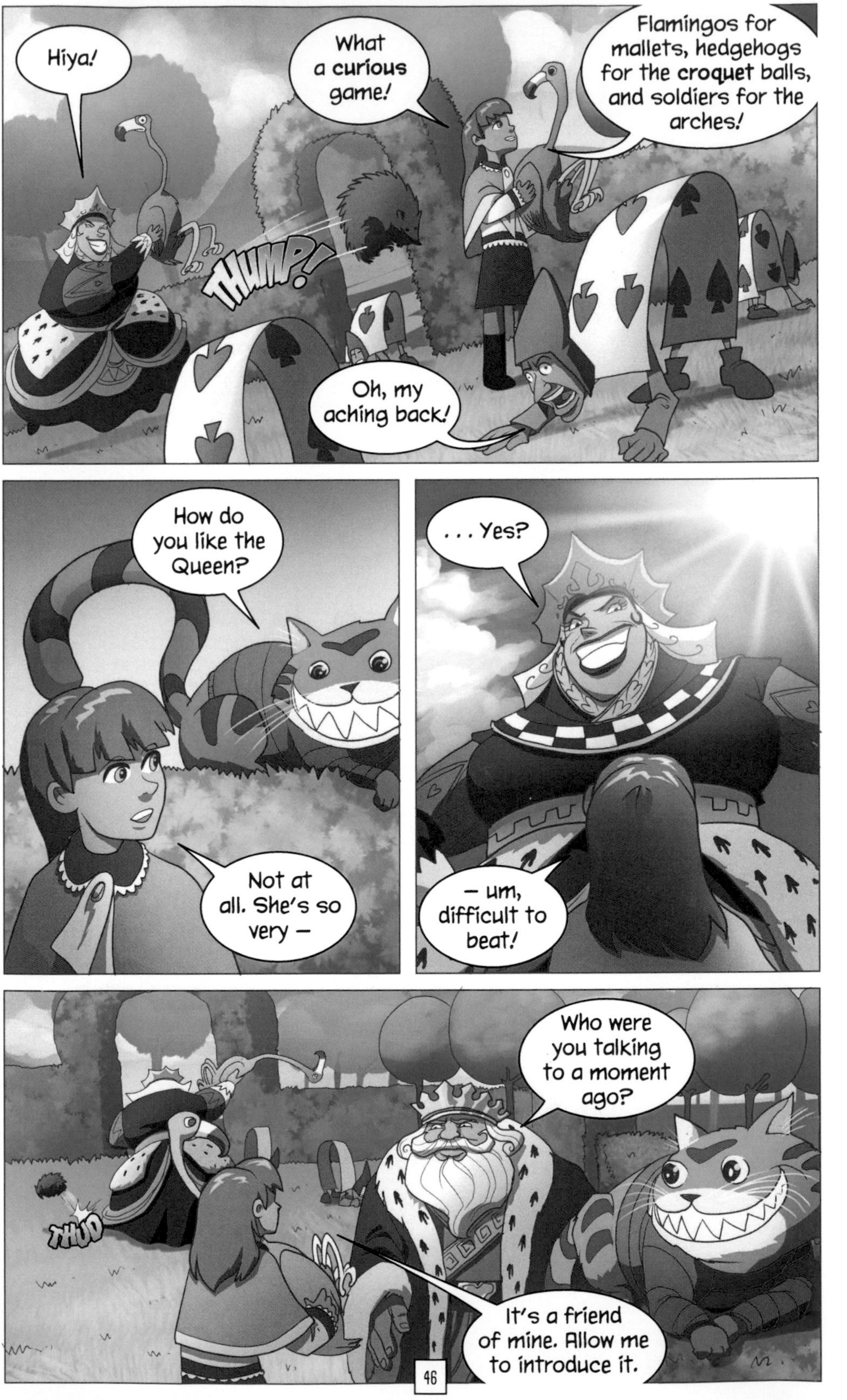
Hiya!
What a curious game!
Flamingos for mallets, hedgehogs for the croquet balls, and soldiers for the arches!
THUMP!
Oh, my aching back!
How do you like the Queen?
Not at all. She's so very –
. . . Yes?
– um, difficult to beat!
Who were you talking to a moment ago?
THUD
It's a friend of mine. Allow me to introduce it.

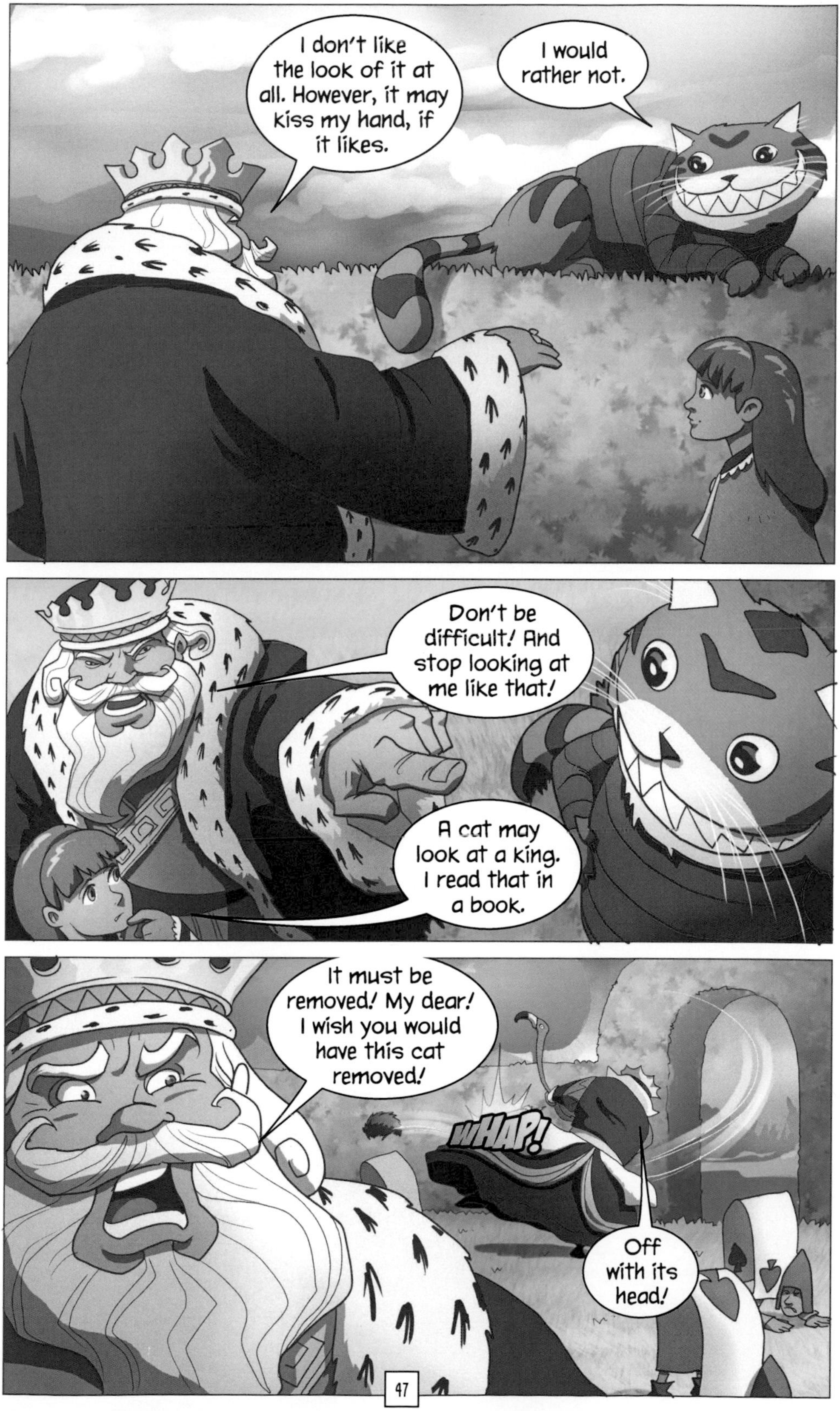
I don't like the look of it at all. However, it may kiss my hand, if it likes.
I would rather not.
Don't be difficult! And stop looking at me like that!
A cat may look at a king. I read that in a book.
It must be removed! My dear! I wish you would have this cat removed!
WHAP!
Off with its head!

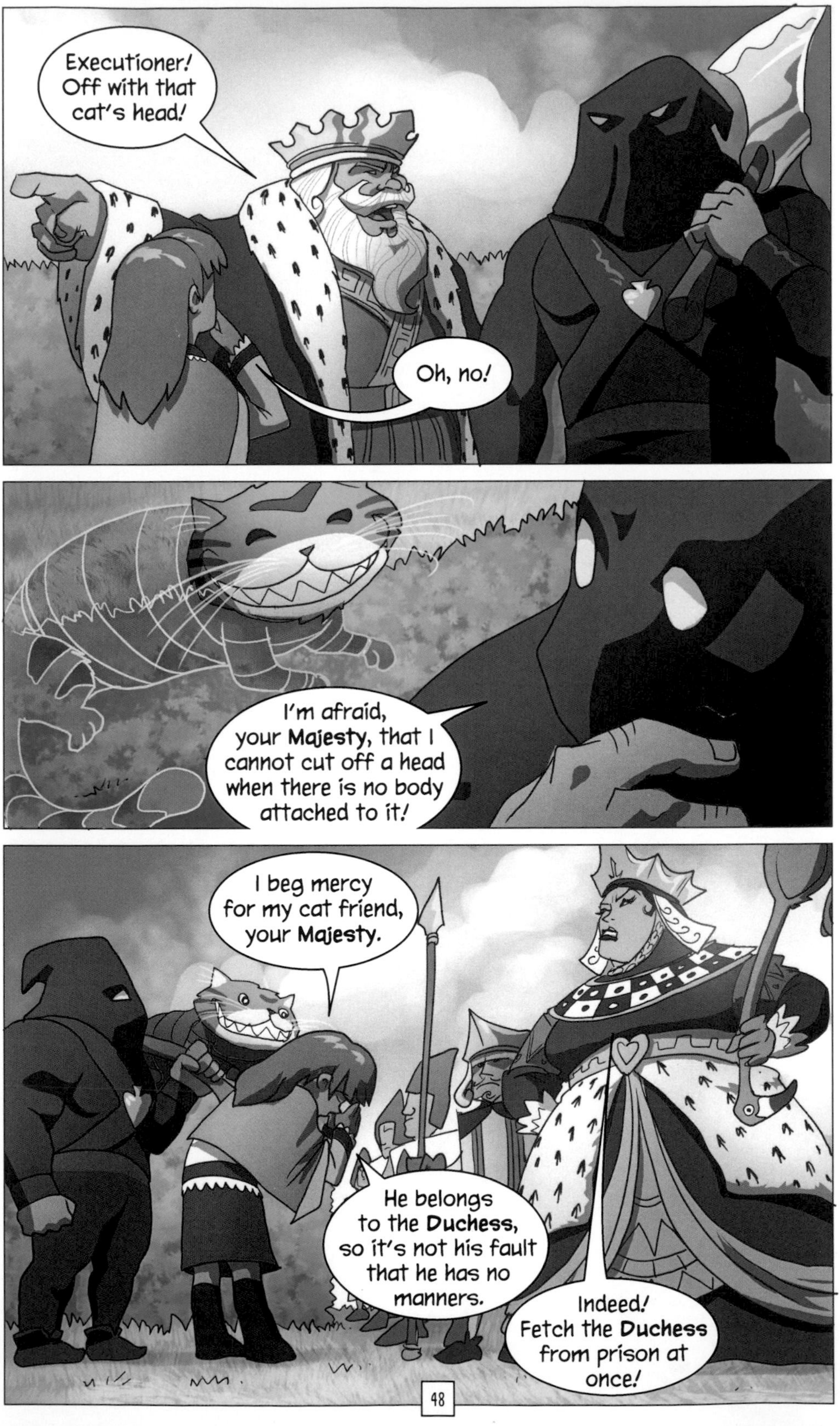
Executioner! Off with that cat's head!
Oh, no!
I'm afraid, your Majesty, that I cannot cut off a head when there is no body attached to it!
I beg mercy for my cat friend, your Majesty.
He belongs to the Duchess, so it's not his fault that he has no manners.
Indeed! Fetch the Duchess from prison at once!

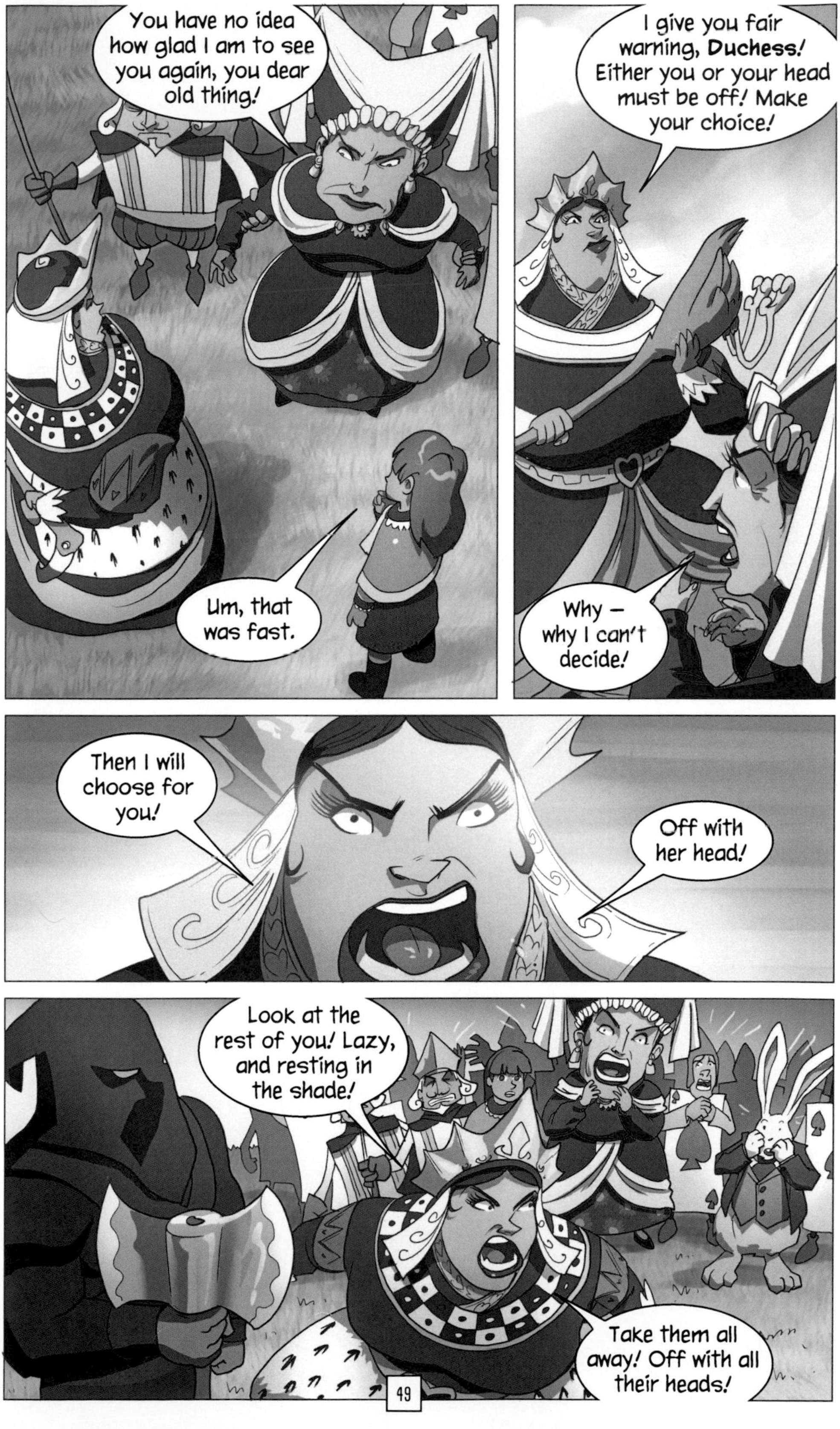
You have no idea how glad I am to see you again, you dear old thing!
Um, that was fast.
I give you fair warning, **Duchess!** Either you or your head must be off! Make your choice!
Why – why I can't decide!
Then I will choose for you!
Off with her head!
Look at the rest of you! Lazy, and resting in the shade!
Take them all away! Off with all their heads!

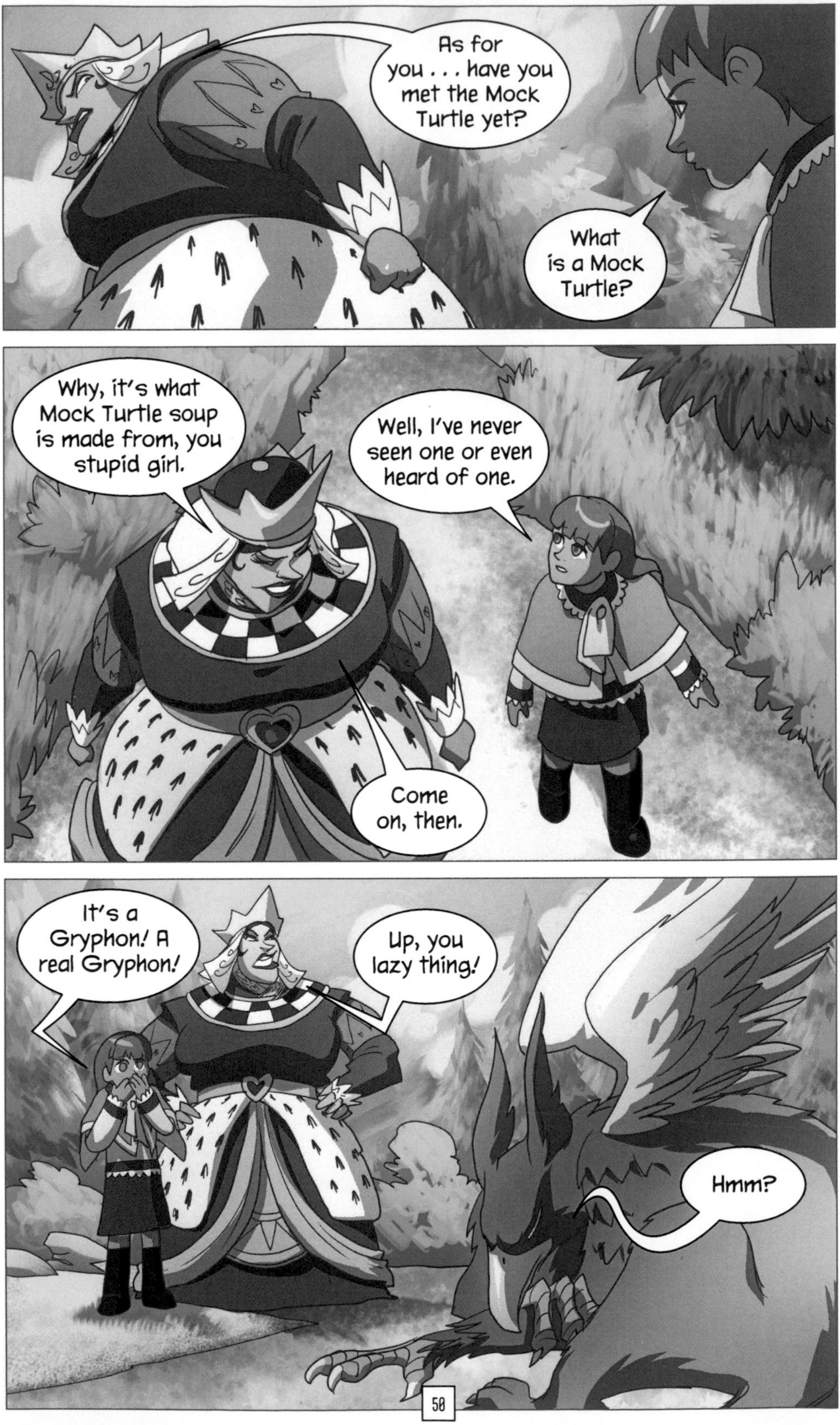
As for you . . . have you met the Mock Turtle yet?
What is a Mock Turtle?
Why, it's what Mock Turtle soup is made from, you stupid girl.
Well, I've never seen one or even heard of one.
Come on, then.
It's a Gryphon! A real Gryphon!
Up, you lazy thing!
Hmm?

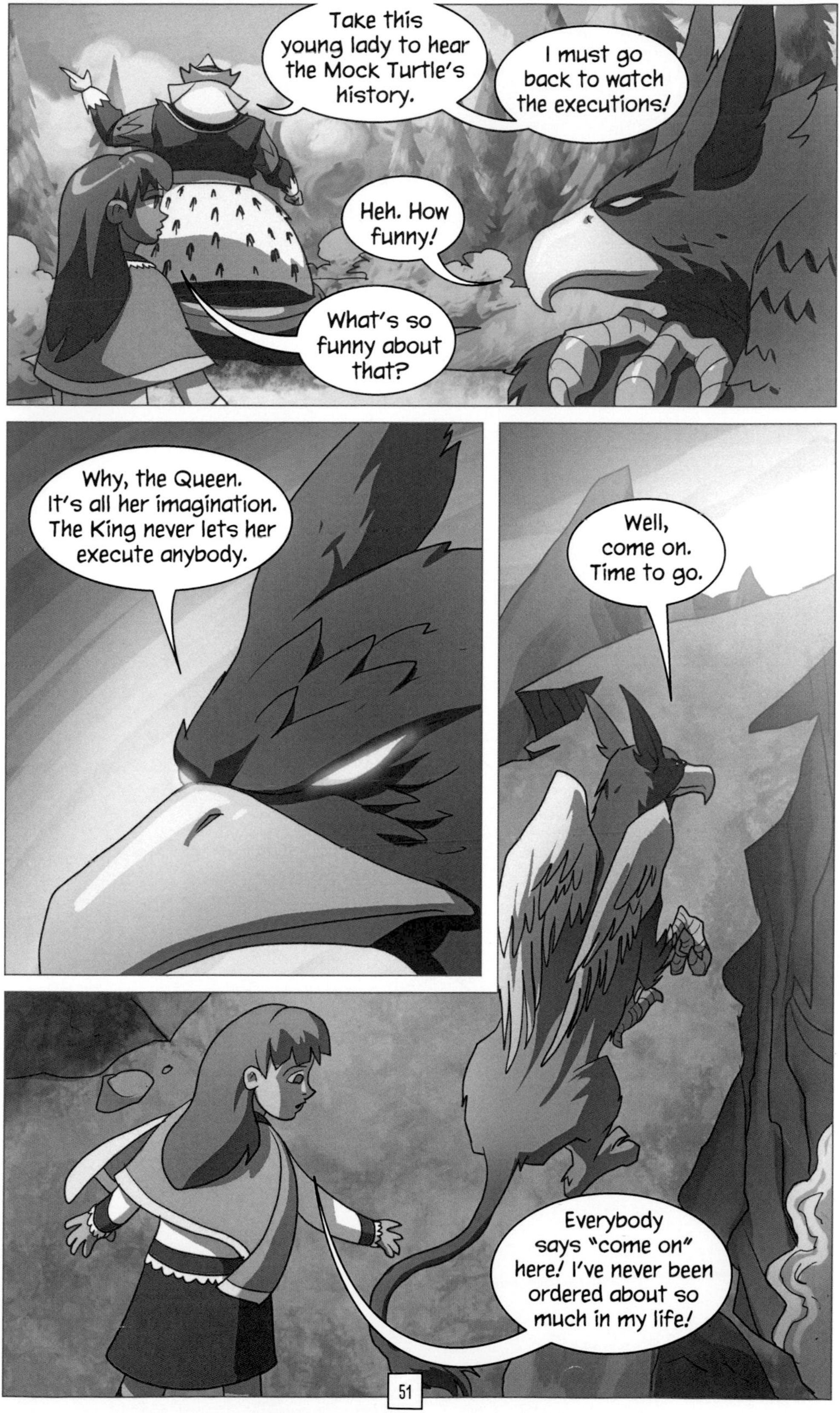
Take this young lady to hear the Mock Turtle's history.
I must go back to watch the executions!
Heh. How funny!
What's so funny about that?
Why, the Queen. It's all her imagination. The King never lets her execute anybody.
Well, come on. Time to go.
Everybody says "come on" here! I've never been ordered about so much in my life!

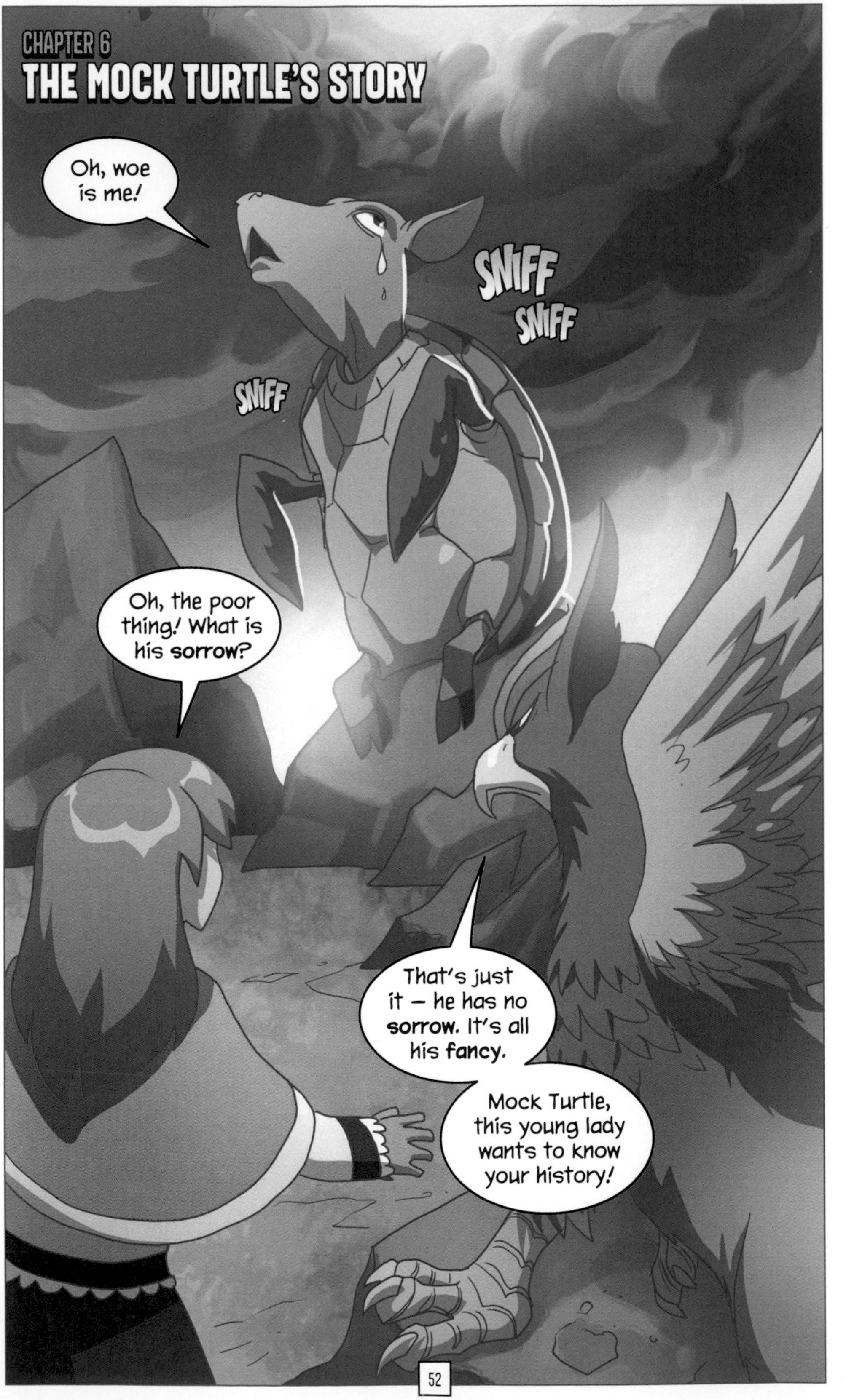
CHAPTER 6
THE MOCK TURTLE'S STORY
Oh, woe is me!
SNIFF
SNIFF
SNIFF
Oh, the poor thing! What is his sorrow?
That's just it — he has no sorrow. It's all his fancy.
Mock Turtle, this young lady wants to know your history!

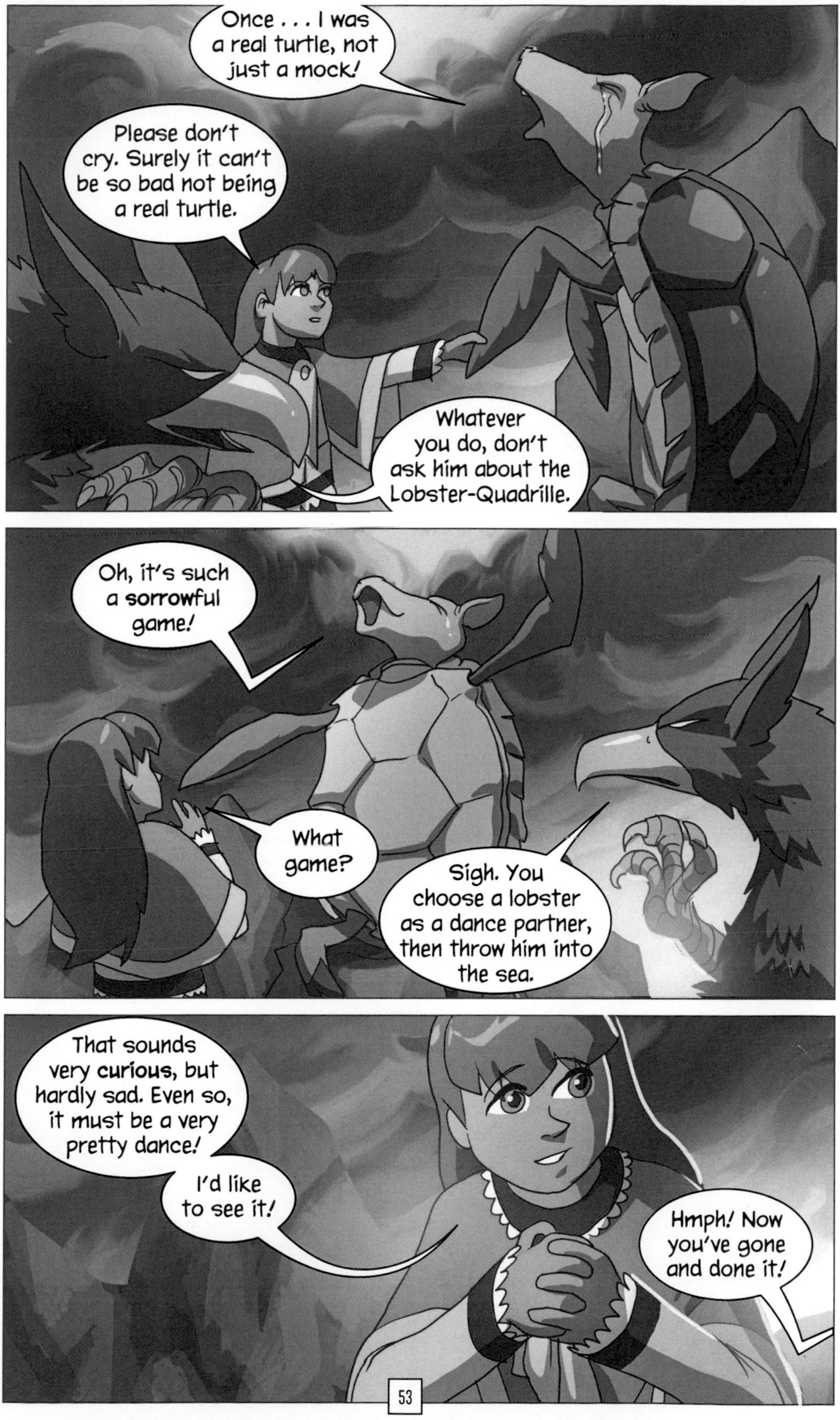
Once . . . I was a real turtle, not just a mock!
Please don't cry. Surely it can't be so bad not being a real turtle.
Whatever you do, don't ask him about the Lobster-Quadrille.
Oh, it's such a **sorrowful** game!
What game?
Sigh. You choose a lobster as a dance partner, then throw him into the sea.
That sounds very **curious**, but hardly sad. Even so, it must be a very pretty dance!
I'd like to see it!
Hmph! Now you've gone and done it!

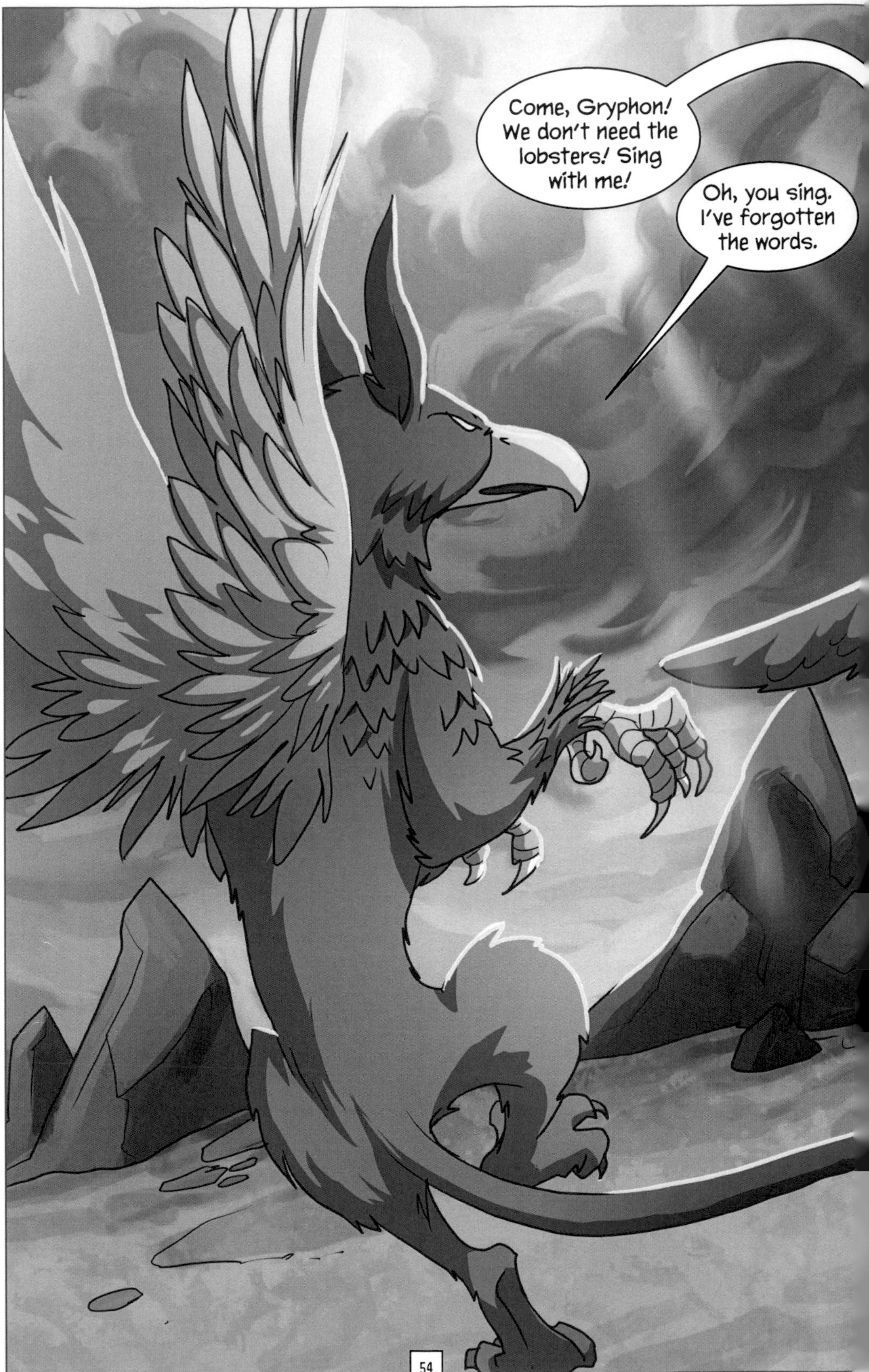
Come, Gryphon! We don't need the lobsters! Sing with me!
Oh, you sing. I've forgotten the words.

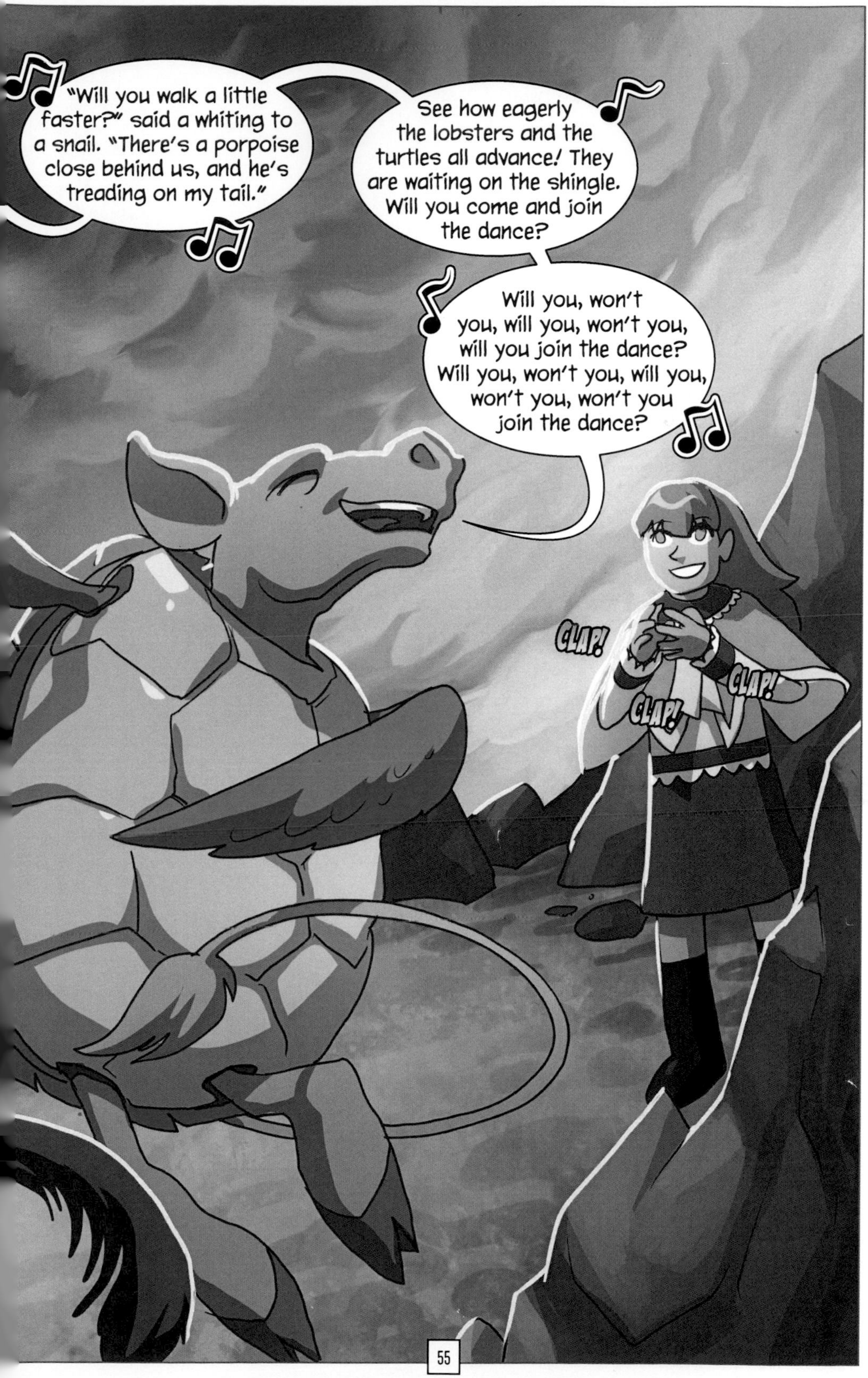
"Will you walk a little faster?" said a whiting to a snail. "There's a porpoise close behind us, and he's treading on my tail."
See how eagerly the lobsters and the turtles all advance! They are waiting on the shingle. Will you come and join the dance?
Will you, won't you, will you, won't you, will you join the dance? Will you, won't you, will you, won't you, won't you join the dance?
CLAP!
CLAP!
CLAP!

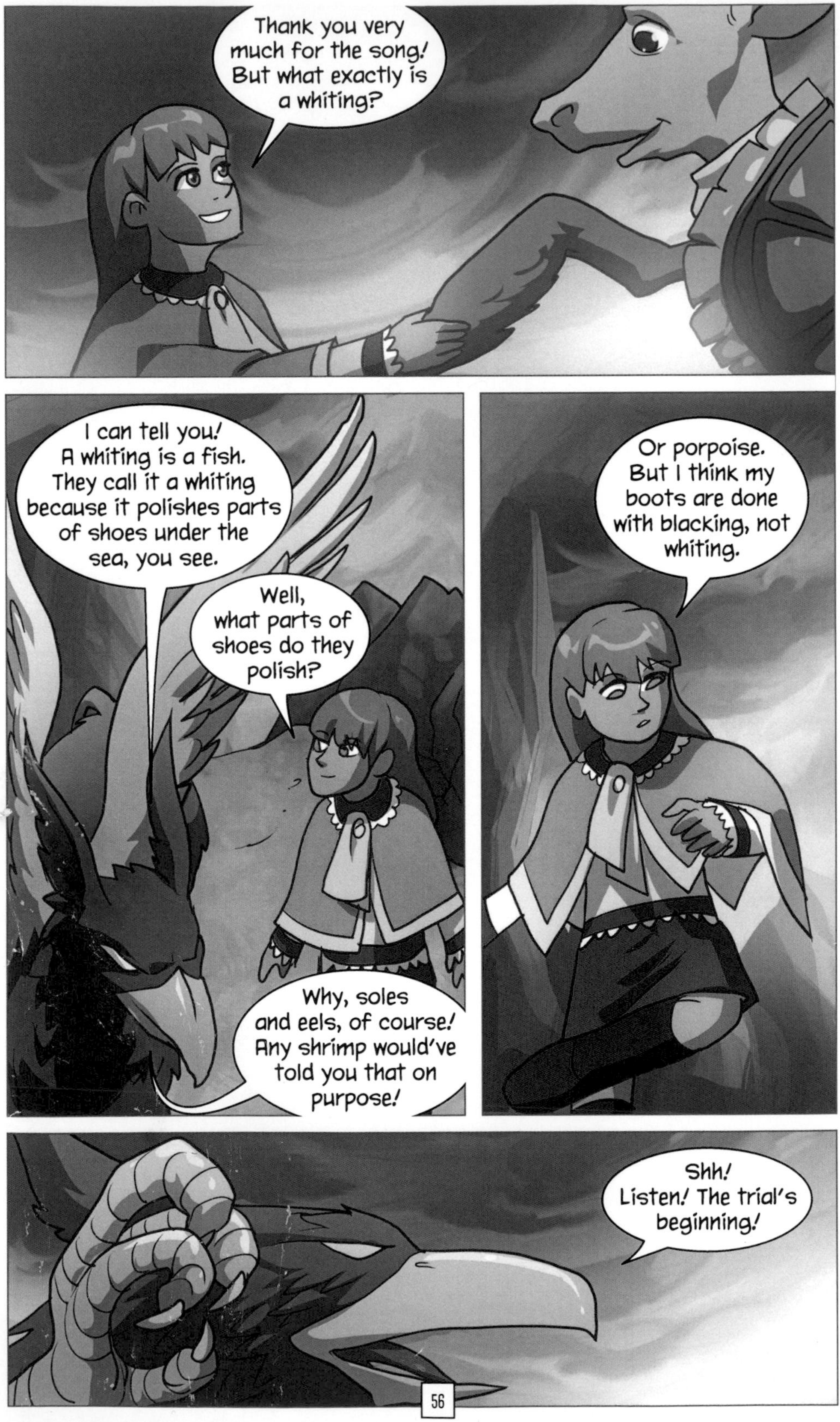
Thank you very much for the song! But what exactly is a whiting?
I can tell you! A whiting is a fish. They call it a whiting because it polishes parts of shoes under the sea, you see.
Well, what parts of shoes do they polish?
Why, soles and eels, of course! Any shrimp would've told you that on purpose!
Or porpoise. But I think my boots are done with blacking, not whiting.
Shh! Listen! The trial's beginning!

# CHAPTER 7
# ALICE'S EVIDENCE

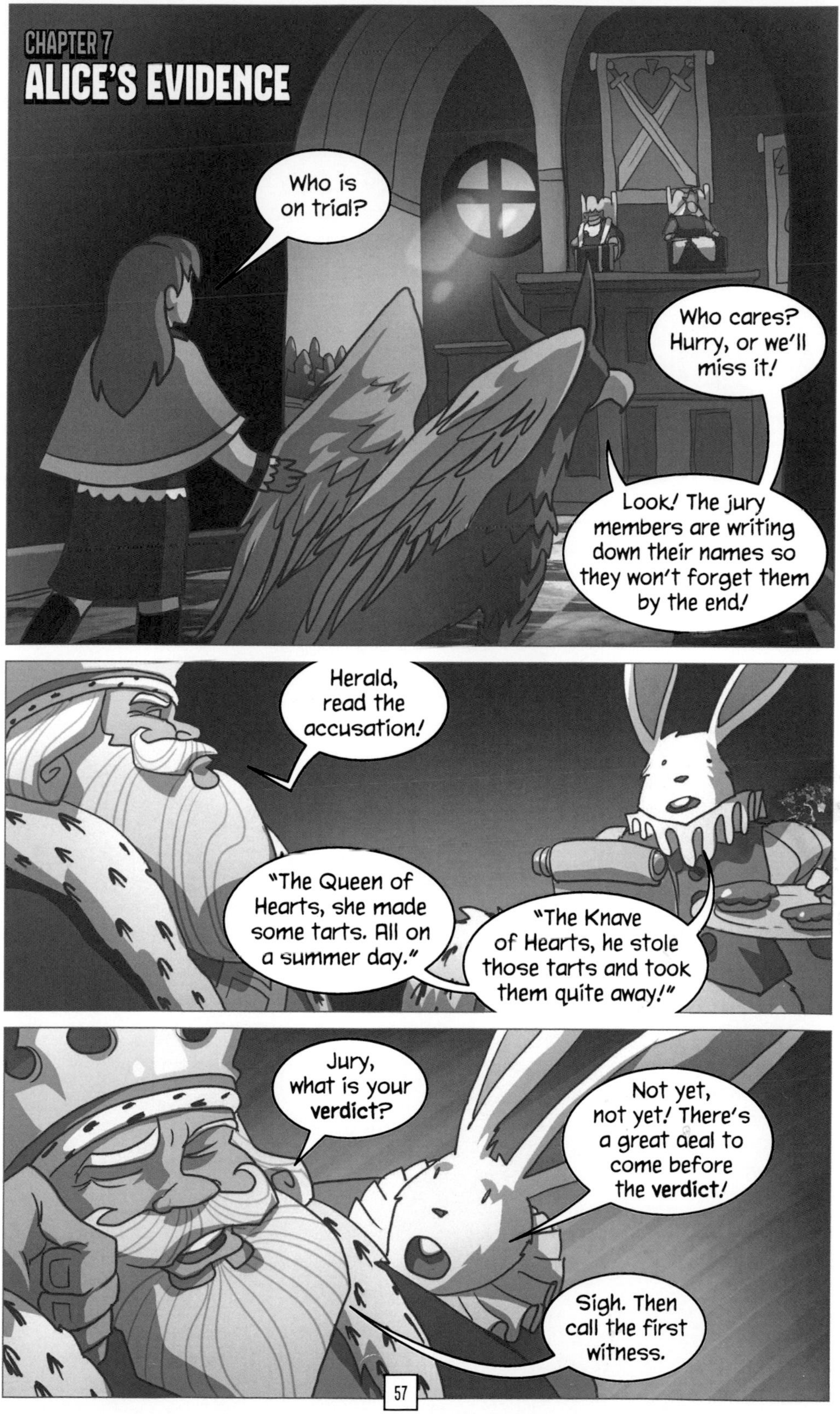
Who is on trial?
Who cares? Hurry, or we'll miss it!
Look! The jury members are writing down their names so they won't forget them by the end!
Herald, read the accusation!
"The Queen of Hearts, she made some tarts. All on a summer day."
"The Knave of Hearts, he stole those tarts and took them quite away!"
Jury, what is your **verdict**?
Not yet, not yet! There's a great deal to come before the **verdict**!
Sigh. Then call the first witness.

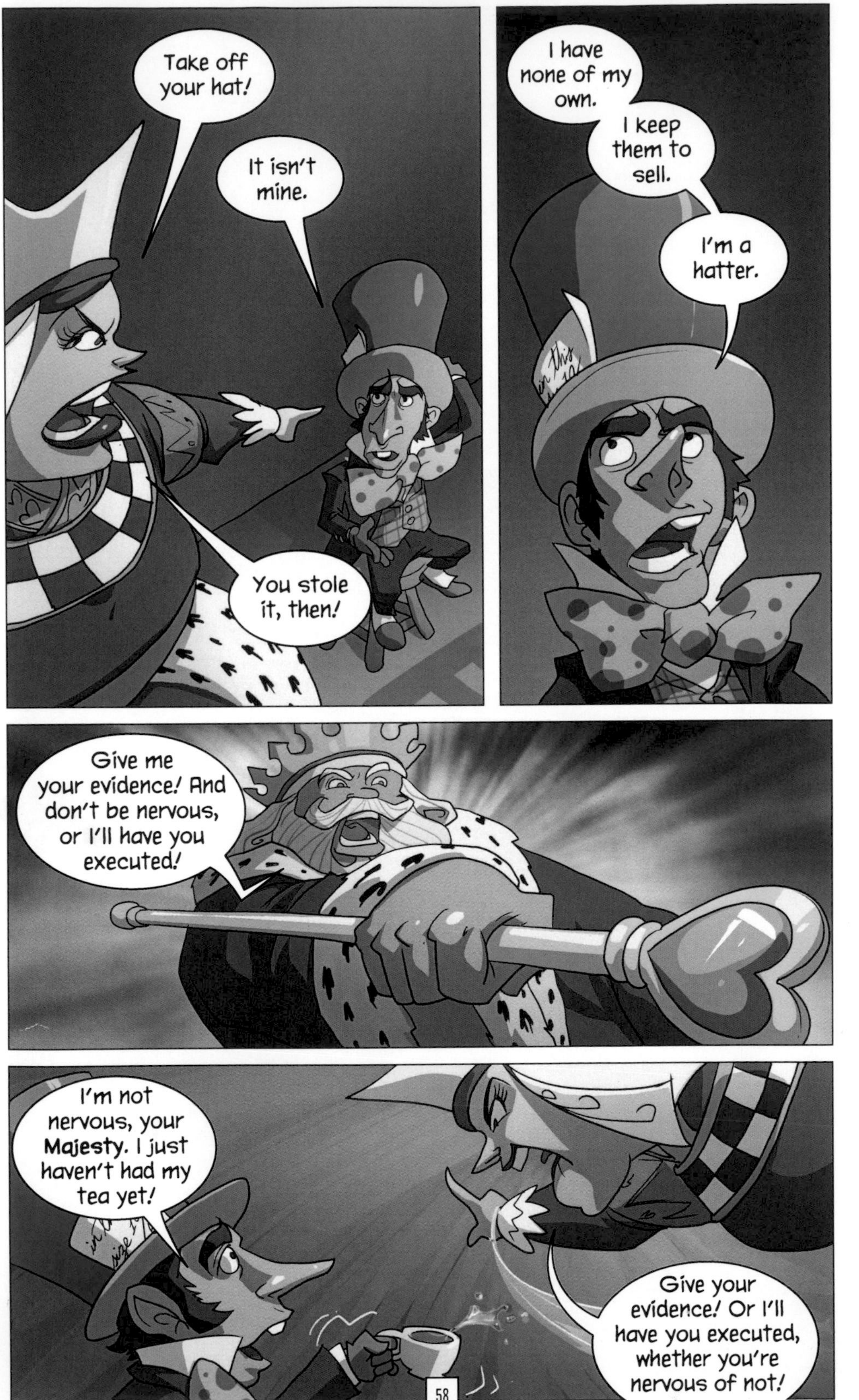
Take off your hat!
It isn't mine.
You stole it, then!
I have none of my own.
I keep them to sell.
I'm a hatter.
Give me your evidence! And don't be nervous, or I'll have you executed!
I'm not nervous, your **Majesty**. I just haven't had my tea yet!
Give your evidence! Or I'll have you executed, whether you're nervous of not!

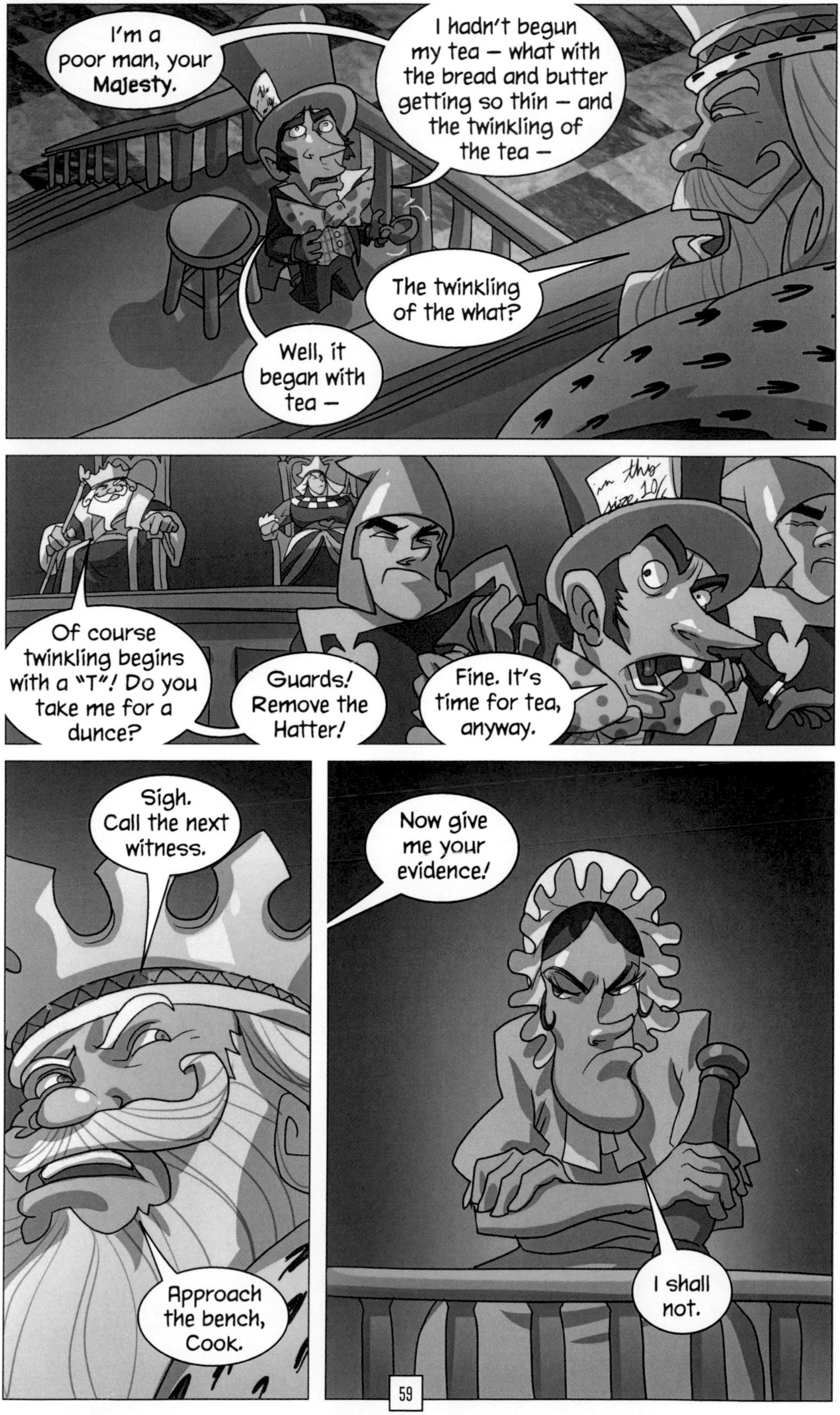
I'm a poor man, your Majesty.
I hadn't begun my tea – what with the bread and butter getting so thin – and the twinkling of the tea –
The twinkling of the what?
Well, it began with tea –
Of course twinkling begins with a "T"! Do you take me for a dunce?
Guards! Remove the Hatter!
Fine. It's time for tea, anyway.
Sigh. Call the next witness.
Approach the bench, Cook.
Now give me your evidence!
I shall not.

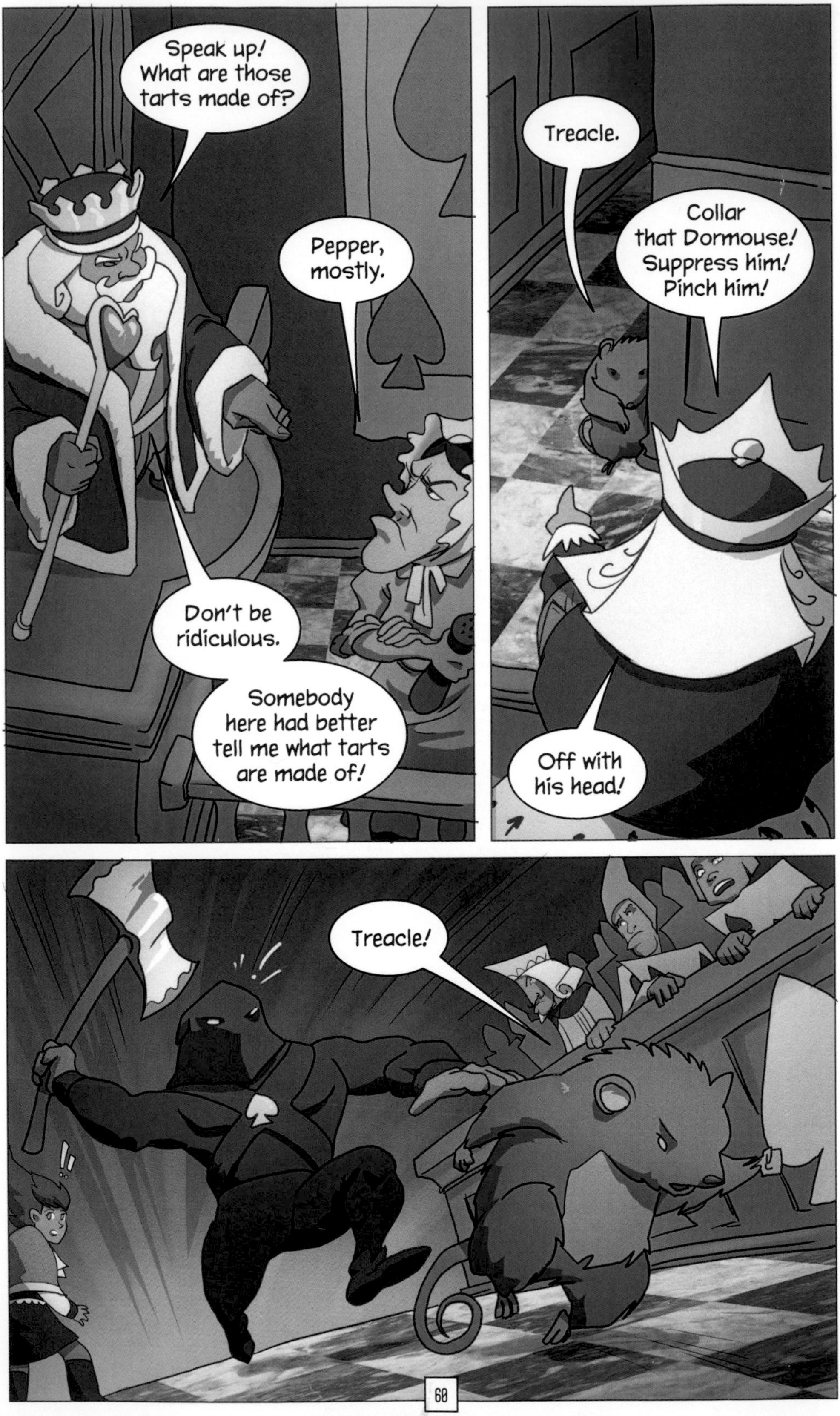
Speak up! What are those tarts made of?
Pepper, mostly.
Don't be ridiculous.
Somebody here had better tell me what tarts are made of!
Treacle.
Collar that Dormouse! Suppress him! Pinch him!
Off with his head!
Treacle!

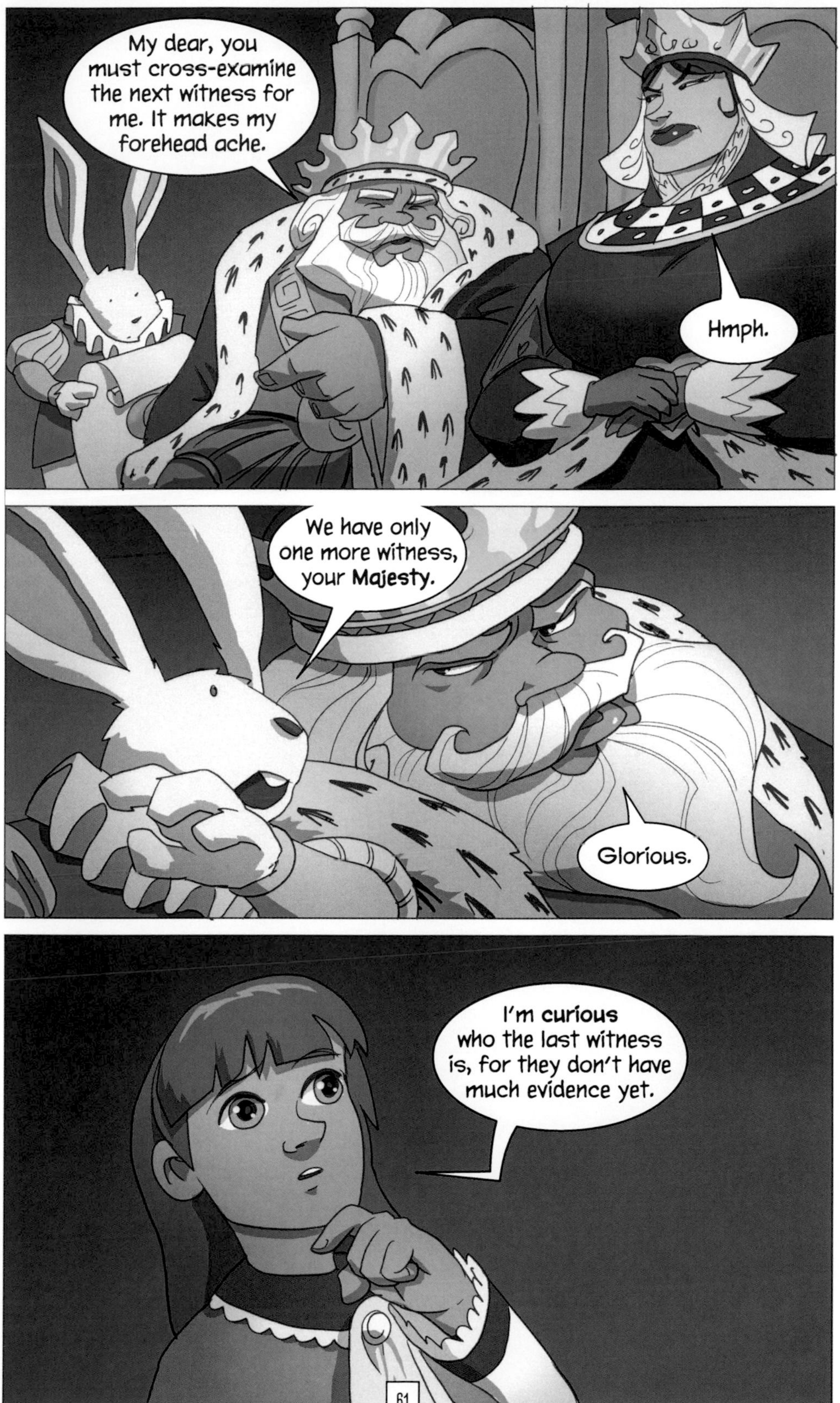
My dear, you must cross-examine the next witness for me. It makes my forehead ache.
Hmph.
We have only one more witness, your **Majesty**.
Glorious.
I'm **curious** who the last witness is, for they don't have much evidence yet.

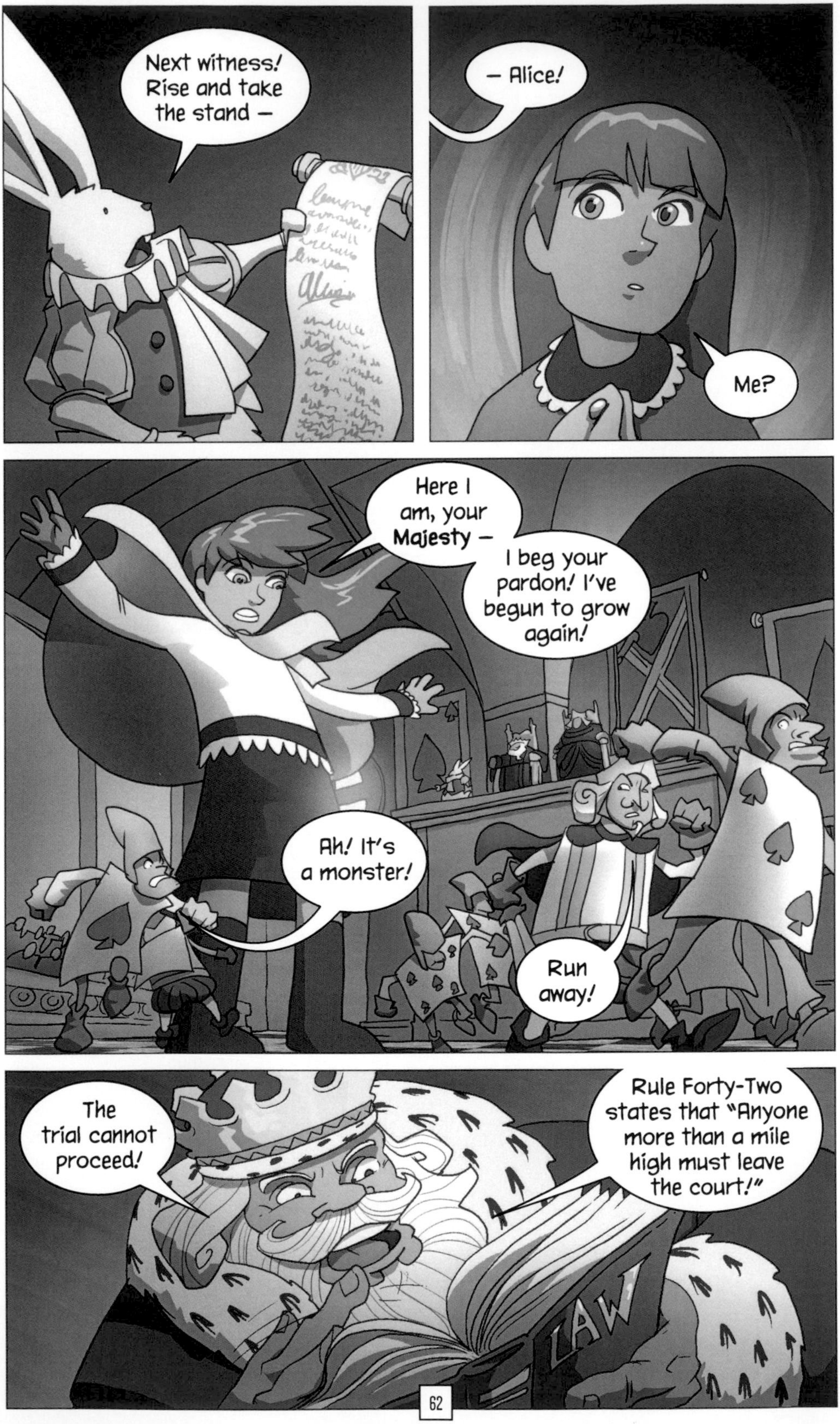
Next witness! Rise and take the stand –
– Alice!
Me?
Here I am, your **Majesty** –
I beg your pardon! I've begun to grow again!
Ah! It's a monster!
Run away!
The trial cannot proceed!
Rule Forty-Two states that "Anyone more than a mile high must leave the court!"
LAW

I'm not a mile high!
Yes you are!
You're nearly two miles high!
Well, anyway, I won't go. That's not a regular rule. You just made it up.
It's the oldest rule in the book!
Off with her head!
Let the jury consider their **verdict**!

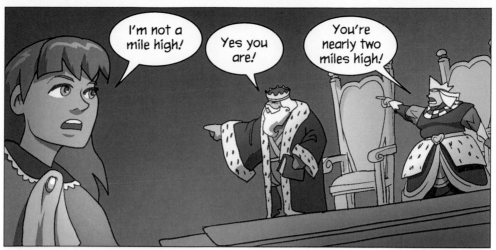

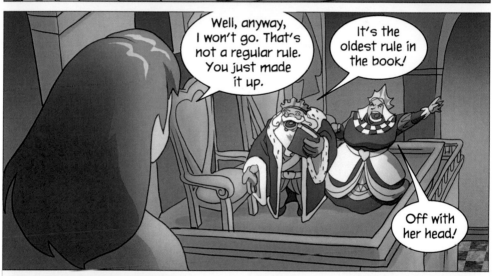

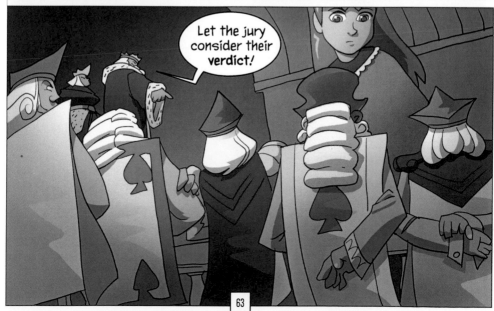

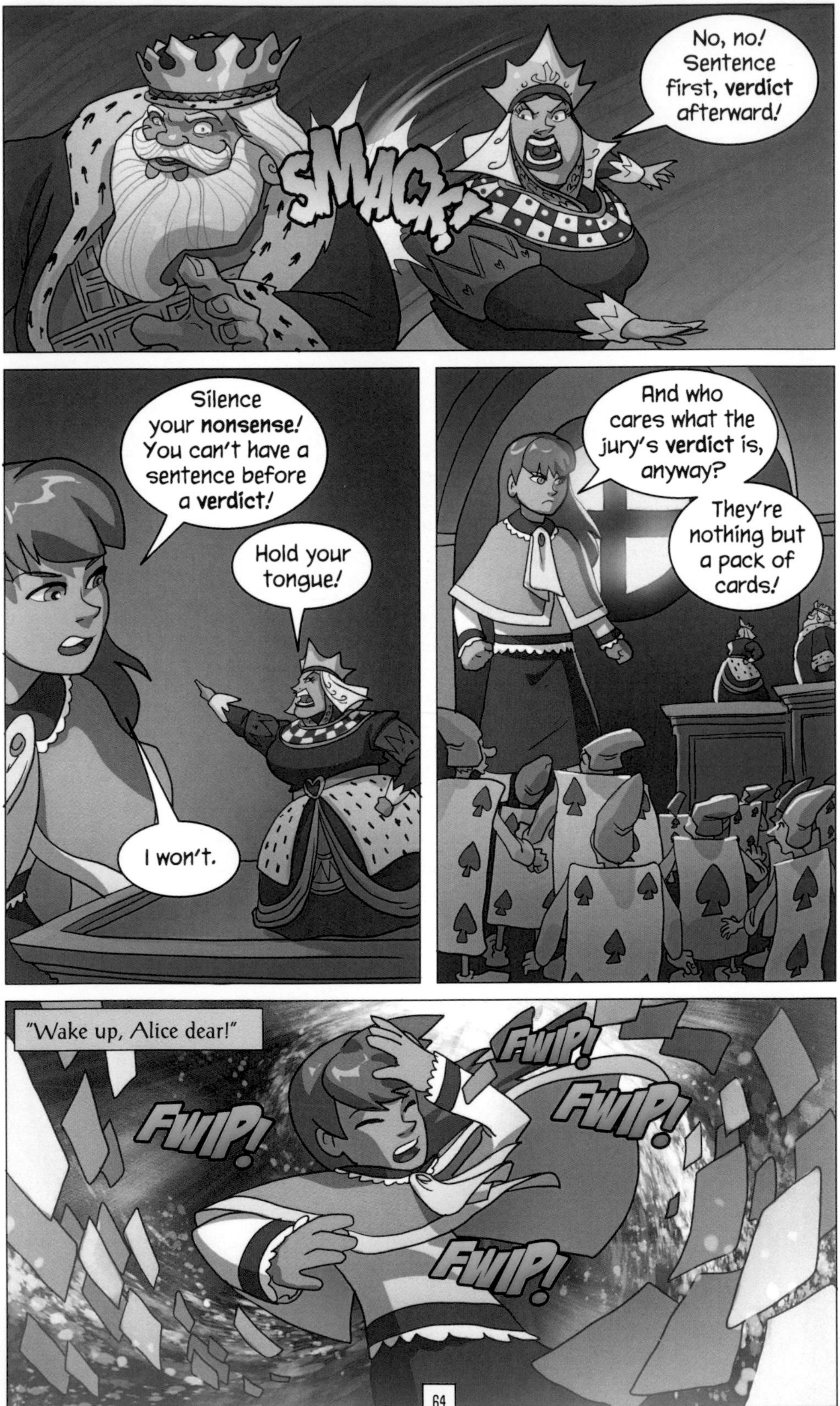
SMACK!
No, no! Sentence first, verdict afterward!
Silence your nonsense! You can't have a sentence before a verdict!
Hold your tongue!
I won't.
And who cares what the jury's verdict is, anyway?
They're nothing but a pack of cards!
"Wake up, Alice dear!"
FWIP!
FWIP!
FWIP!
FWIP!

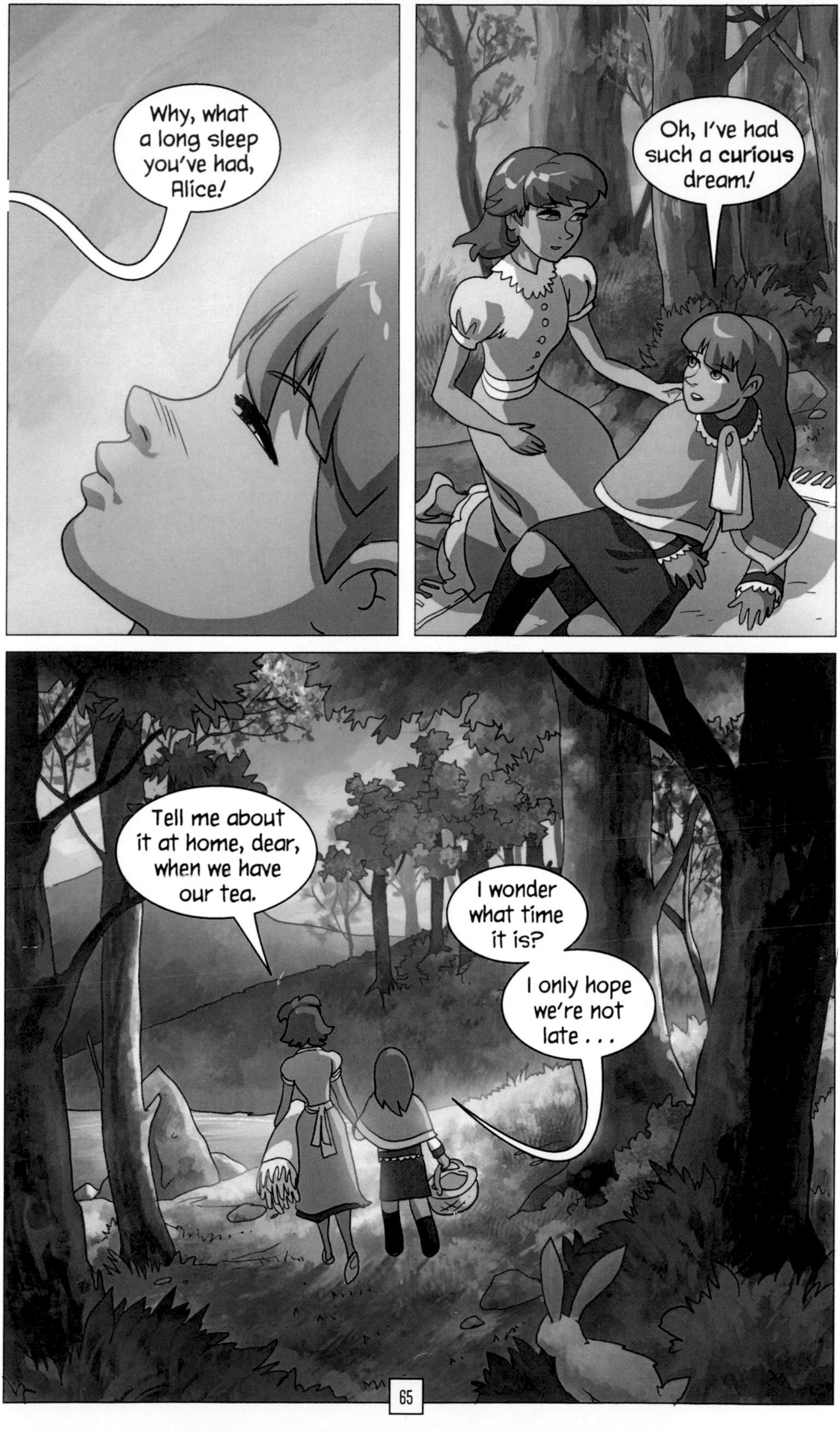
Why, what a long sleep you've had, Alice!
Oh, I've had such a **curious** dream!
Tell me about it at home, dear, when we have our tea.
I wonder what time it is?
I only hope we're not late . . .

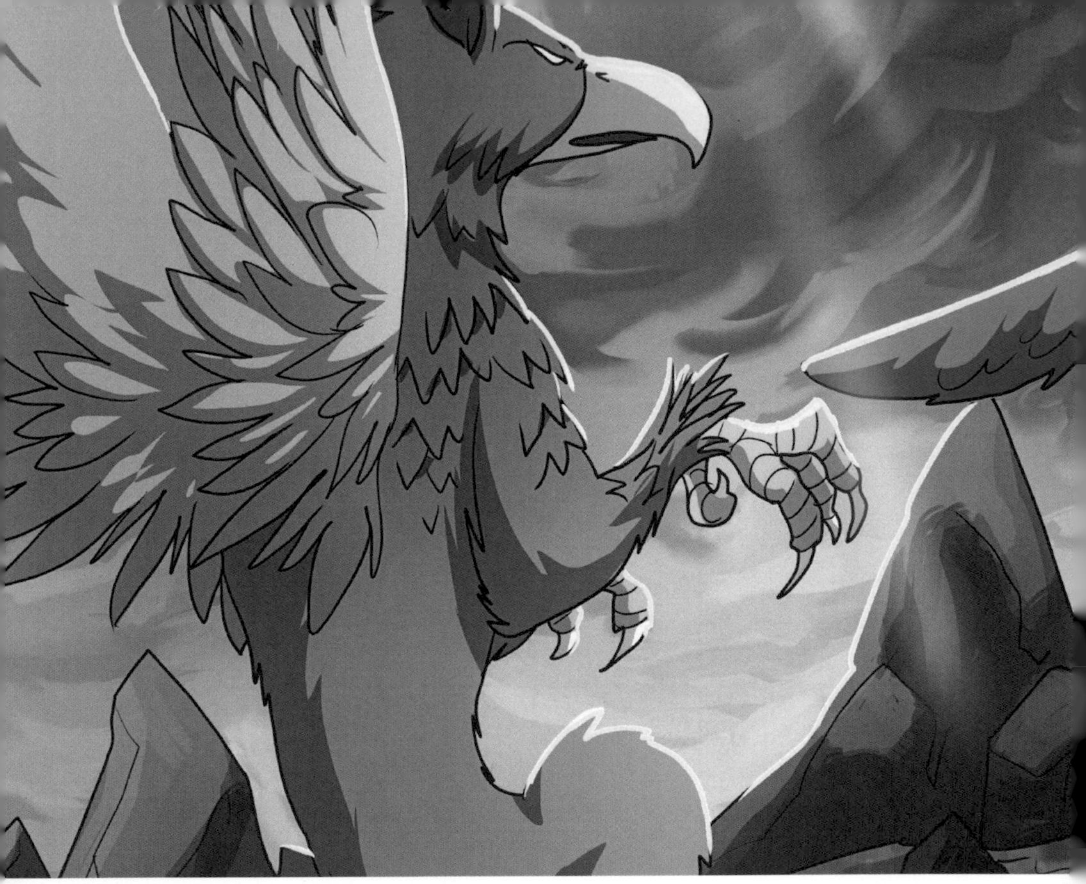

# ABOUT THE RETELLING AUTHOR AND ILLUSTRATOR

Since 1986, author **Martin Powell** has been a freelance writer. He has written hundreds of stories, many of which have been published by Disney, Marvel, Tekno Comix, Moonstone Books, and others. In 1989, Powell received an Eisner Award nomination for his graphic novel *Scarlet in Gaslight*. This award is one of the highest comic book honors.

Illustrator **Daniel Ferran** was born in Monterrey, Mexico, in 1977. For more than a decade, Daniel has worked as a colorist and an illustrator for comic book publishers such as Marvel, Image, and Dark Horse. He currently works for Protobunker Studio.

# GLOSSARY

**absurdly** (ab-SURD-lee)—in a silly or ridiculous way

**caucus** (KAW-kuhss)—a group or meeting intended to further a cause

**croquet** (kroh-KAY)—an outdoor game played by hitting wooden balls with mallets through wire hoops

**curious** (KYUR-ee-uhss)—strange or odd

**duchess** (DUHCH-iss)—the wife or widow of a duke

**fancy** (FAN-see)—imagination

**mad** (MAD)—insane or crazy

**majesty** (MAJ-uh-stee)—a formal title for a ruler

**nonsense** (NON-senss)—silliness or meaninglessness

**pity** (PIT-ee)—feeling sorry for someone or something

**sorrow** (SAH-roh)—great sadness

**verdict** (VUR-dikt)—a jury's decision of guilt or innocence

# COMMON CORE ALIGNED
# READING QUESTIONS

1. On the very first page of Alice in Wonderland, Alice says, "I don't understand how you can read that old book. There aren't even any pictures." In what ways is this quote significant to the rest of the story?" ("*Refer to details and examples in a text when explaining what the text says explicitly and when drawing inferences from the text.*")

2. What is Alice like as a person in the beginning of the story? What does she learn by the end of the story? ("*Describe in depth a character, setting, or event in a story.*")

3. "Wonder" is not only in the title of this graphic novel, but it is also a major theme. Try to find every page that uses the word "wonder" and explain why "wonder" is used in each example. ("*Determine a theme of a story.*")

4. Why is the rabbit significant to the story? What is his purpose? ("*Describe in depth a character . . . drawing on specific details in the text.*")

5. The settings in this graphic novel are interesting and well illustrated. What does the King and Queen's castle look like? What does it look like inside? Outside? How does the setting reflect the King and Queen's personalities? ("*Refer to details and examples in a text when explaining what the text says explicitly and when drawing inferences from the text.*")

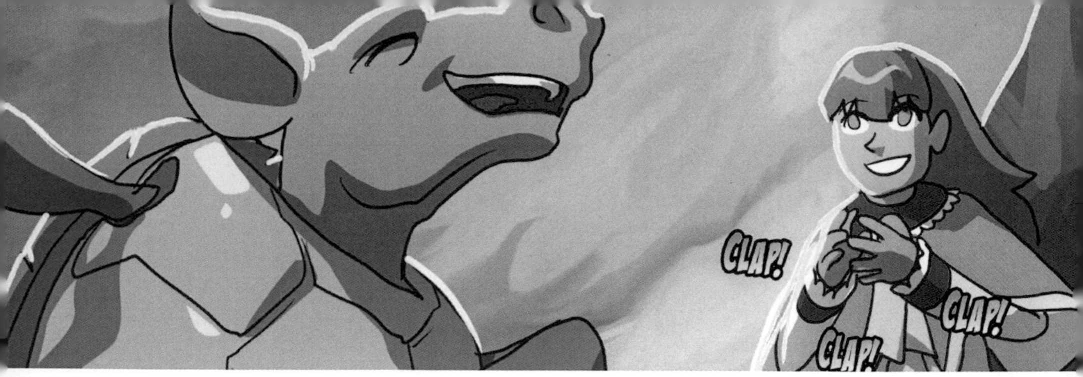
CLAP!
CLAP!
CLAP!

COMMON CORE ALIGNED
# WRITING QUESTIONS

1. **Is the Chesire Cat a reliable character? Why or why not? Write a paragraph explaining your answer. Use evidence from the text and the illustrations to support your opinion.** *("Write opinion pieces on topics or texts, supporting a point of view with reasons and information.")*

2. **Write a reflection essay on each step of Alice's journey into Wonderland. What happens, and in what order?** *("Produce clear and coherent writing in which the development and organization are appropriate to task, purpose, and audience.")*

3. **Write down three adjectives to describe Wonderland. Next to each adjective, explain why you chose that particular word. Make sure to reference words and/or illustrations that support your answers.** *("Write informative/explanatory texts to examine a topic and convey ideas.")*

4. **Personification plays an important role in this book. Personification is when something that is not human comes alive and acts like a human. If you could personify one of the King and Queen's playing-card guards, what would the card say to Alice about the King and Queen of Hearts?** *("Write narratives to develop real or imagined experiences or events.")*

5. **Pretend you are Alice. Write a letter home to explain where you are and what is happening.** *("Produce clear and coherent writing in which the development and organization are appropriate to task, purpose, and audience.")*

# READ THEM ALL!

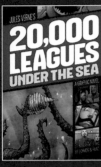

JULES VERNE'S
**20,000 LEAGUES UNDER THE SEA**
A GRAPHIC NOVEL

MARK TWAIN'S
**THE ADVENTURES OF TOM SAWYER**
A GRAPHIC NOVEL

ANNA SEWELL'S
**BLACK BEAUTY**
A GRAPHIC NOVEL

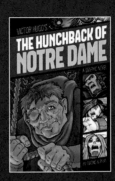

VICTOR HUGO'S
**THE HUNCHBACK OF NOTRE DAME**
A GRAPHIC NOVEL

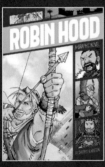

**ROBIN HOOD**
A GRAPHIC NOVEL

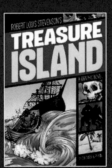

ROBERT LOUIS STEVENSON'S
**TREASURE ISLAND**
A GRAPHIC NOVEL

MARY SHELLEY'S
**FRANKENSTEIN**
A GRAPHIC NOVEL

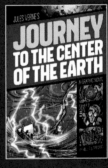

JULES VERNE'S
**JOURNEY TO THE CENTER OF THE EARTH**
A GRAPHIC NOVEL

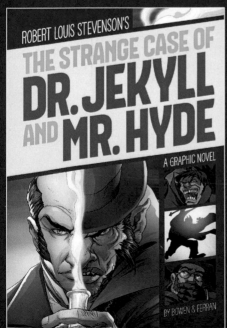

ROBERT LOUIS STEVENSON'S
**THE STRANGE CASE OF DR. JEKYLL AND MR. HYDE**
A GRAPHIC NOVEL
BY BOWEN & FERRAN

WASHINGTON IRVING'S
**THE LEGEND OF SLEEPY HOLLOW**
A GRAPHIC NOVEL

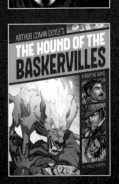

**DRACULA**

JONATHAN SWIFT'S
**GULLIVER'S TRAVELS**
A GRAPHIC NOVEL

ARTHUR CONAN DOYLE'S
**THE HOUND OF THE BASKERVILLES**
A GRAPHIC NOVEL

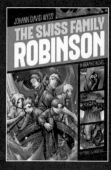

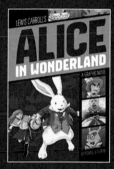
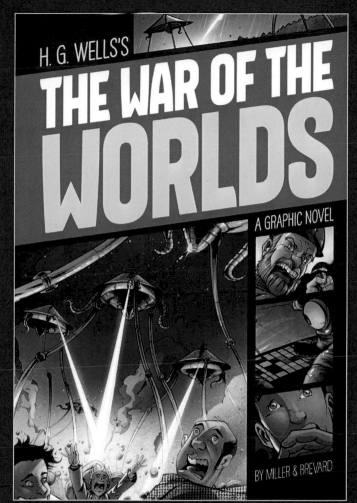

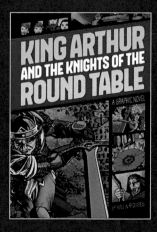
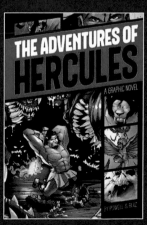